DEADLY VOWS

A Cree Blue Psychic Eye Mystery Book 2

Kate Allenton

Published by Coastal Escape
Publishing

Discover other titles by Kate Allenton
At

http://www.kateallenton.com

ISBN- 978-1-944237-46-2

DEADLY VOWS

Chapter 1

"Tell me you're going to put a hex on him or send a poltergeist to his new apartment," Freddie demanded as I ended my call.
He was leaning against the old doorframe of my ancestral home. The bald opinionated Italian was my self-appointed bodyguard, so I gave him latitude. It was that or have to deal with the rest of the Italian mob knocking some sense into my poor delicate head. I already had enough loose screws; I couldn't afford many more.

The Lady Blue Plantation served as more than my serenity. Its vast open yards and ancient trees calmed me in a way no other place came close to doing. It was one reason I believe people were drawn to it. Freddie was one of those people I let live under my roof. Most people would be scared to have an Italian ex-mobster sleeping down the hall. Not me. It helped me sleep.

"I'm not a witch." Not that I couldn't pay $19.95 for someone on the internet to do the deed. Bad karma wasn't juju to be toyed with, ever. "He's just busy."

Freddie's observant well-trained laser focus pinned me in my spot. I guess his time dealing with double-crossing bad guys who could kill kind of made him paranoid that way. Regardless, he had a point. Two months and my *almost* relationship with FBI Agent Mason Spencer had disappeared like last night's pitcher of margaritas. His new job with the FBI kept him MIA and emotionally off the radar.

"He's busy all right; busy avoiding you."

Deep down in the pit of my stomach, somewhere between last night's burrito and this morning's piece of chocolate cake, I knew Freddie was right, and that thought irked me even more than my nonexistent boyfriend.

"Fine, he's avoiding me." I frowned. "He isn't the only one."

West Archer was doing the same thing. The British agent had shown up two months ago seeking help with the case of the century; a dead actress, a royal affair, and a missing diamond worth a small fortune. He dangled that case like a freakin' dessert in front of a woman on a diet before he disappeared. The men in my life had a problem keeping their word.

"Screw them, Cree. It's their loss. You're the rock star. You talk to dead people and help solve cold cases that people like them can't figure out. Mason is probably just sitting behind some desk talking about the merits of which shoulder holster doesn't chafe, and Archer, God only knows where he went, but one thing is for sure. You're the one doing all the work."

"Work," I sighed. "I guess they're ready and waiting for us?"

"You could say that."

"I almost forgot we planned to work a case." I shoved to my feet.

"Pity parties tend to do that." Freddie chuckled and rested his arm on my shoulder, steering me back inside where the others waited.

My pity party wasn't over. I'd simply pressed pause until I could be alone with a glass of wine and a pint of my favorite chocolate ice cream.

I walked into the ballroom, shoving all thoughts of Mason and his excuses out of my head. The large room was empty other than the tools we'd need. Several desks with computers lined the walls. The big Jumbotron-sized screens hanging on the walls sat idle in standby mode, ready to flash the images from my mind. A hospital bed sat in the middle of the room with Doc Stone hovering nearby to monitor the machines and ready to check my vitals. Everything was ready, except me.

"Sorry to keep you guys waiting."

"Did Freddie talk you off the ledge?" Charlotte, my best friend and partner in crime, asked from her perch behind one of the computers where she was playing a game of solitaire.

"It wasn't a ledge, just a minor speed bump," I said, entering the room. I slid out of my heels, leaving them by the door. "I'm ready to focus."

"It's about damn time," Faraday said from across the room. He folded his arms over his chest. His naturally grumpy annoyance was even more exaggerated today.

He was my personal liaison with the local PD, not to mention my godfather. The way he told it, he was the one that picked my dad up off the floor during my birth, and he's been picking up the pieces ever since.

Insight was my daddy's dream. A computer program that gives everyone in the room a view of the visions going on in my head when trying to tune in to these lost souls who needed to be found. We were all witnesses to the ghastly deeds of the crimes. Whatever I saw in my head, they'd see on the screens. I was the conduit for these dark, deadly deeds.

Only the people in this room knew I used this secret machine to prevent me from missing a clue. They worked like the logical side of my brain while I was using the program.

Jitters was in charge of monitoring and recording everything. He was a computer genius. Charlotte was there for more than moral support. She was wired kind of different, too, which was probably why we're such besties. She could see the connections the rest of us would miss. The twins…well, I think they were just happy to be around like-minded nutty people, and we were a salty bunch.

"Which case are we working on?" Faraday asked. His thinning patience reminded me of rain on a day I wanted to swim; neither warmed my soul. I blew a kiss to the agitated cranky man.

I unlocked the cold case locker of stored evidence the police provided for me to use when trying to connect. Brown bags stacked the shelves, and the case names and file numbers sat out of view. I wouldn't need them.

Closing my eyes, I felt around at the energy each package gave off. When my soul was calm, in tune, I was strong, and I'd work on one of the less energetic pieces. When I was feeling puny, I'd pick the ones with the most active energy. Today, I needed all the help I could get with so much clutter in my brain.

I was immediately drawn to one package on the top shelf. I had no idea what was inside, only that a woman was involved. I jumped to grab it and pull it, catching it in my arms. "Looks like the winner is Davina Richards, Billson Police cold case file 37658."

"That one's more recent. I remember about a month ago the poor girl went missing the day before her wedding. That would be my luck," Charlotte said.

"I'd never let that happen." I grinned and tapped into her energy. "Your Prince Charming is on the way."

"I think he lost his map."

"Ladies, can we focus and leave the girl talk for later?" Faraday said.

"Did you drink too much prune juice today?" I asked and pointed to the kitchen. "We can wait while you go relieve yourself of that bad attitude."

"Funny, Cree."

I shrugged. I had my moments. I glanced again at the name on the bag. I had a vague recollection of seeing something about Davina in the papers. People thought she'd gotten cold feet and taken off, only the police and her fiancé suspected something more devious at work. Call it my intuition or gut feeling, I knew this one wasn't a runaway bride because this chick was already dead. Her apparition was floating just outside the French doors of the ballroom. My Grammy's overbearing ghostly presence kept all of the unrelated dead people out of my house. She was good like that.

I walked across the renovated hardwood floors over to the hospital bed and climbed on top, letting Doc Stone cover me with a blanket. It was a wonder I didn't get many colds. I always start out sweating beneath the fabric until the good Doc pulls out the cold goo. It was all downhill from there. By the time we finish playing with Insight I'd end up needing three more blankets and sometimes even that wouldn't get rid of the chill.

He slipped a rubber cap over my head. To the untrained eye, it looked like something that was used by hairdressers intent on giving highlights, but we used it for something way more interesting.

"This is going to be cold." Doc Stone looked a little hesitant as he approached with the caulking gun filled with cold gel. I hated this part.

"It always is." I tensed as he filled each hole in the cap with the goop, sending a wintry chill crawling down my spine and extending throughout my body. He filled every tiny hole in the cap before attaching the probes the machine needed to transmit the images. Thank God no one ever saw me like this. I looked on the verge of getting a head transplant.

"Whenever you're ready, Cree."

I inhaled a deep, calming breath as I tore open the package, dumping the contents on my lap. I don't know what I'd been expecting, maybe a bloody wedding dress or veil. Instead, it was something much more innocent. A stuffed bear. I held it up for Faraday to see. "Really?"

"The fiancé said she took it with her everywhere. It's the only personal item the Billson PD would give us."

You'd think they'd be a little more accommodating. I was, after all, providing clues they'd yet to find.

"Jitters, are we rolling?" I glanced at the camera he'd just walked away from. The little red flashing dot confirmed my answer before he did.

"Rolling on you, and we're recording the feed. We're a go."

"Okay then, Faraday, if you'll dim the lights." I cleared my throat and leaned back in the bed, nodding to Doc Stone. He flipped the switch. "Davina Richards, Cree Blue Case 55. Billson PD cold case 37658. Let's hunt."

Chapter 2

Images flicked across the screen. First, that of Grammy's wilted rose garden in the backyard I'd been staring at earlier. Then my Grammy's face. Her old wise wrinkles looked amplified on the Jumbotron, calming my rattled nerves. "Let's begin."

I picked up the teddy bear and let the energy cocoon my body, wrap around every bit of my essence, and entwine with mine. It was a weird feeling being so acutely aware of someone else besides myself. Sometimes it was like dropping oil into a bucket of water. Some energy just didn't want to mesh and mix. That wasn't the case with Davina's energy. I gripped the bear tight and let the vibrations whip out of my mind to her last memory, finally focusing on the front of a church.

Davina was holding hands with a man talking to a preacher. Her eyes were unfocused, as if she were in school staring out the window while the teacher lectured on about a subject she hated.

We'll see you at the rehearsal. The guy held out his hand and shook the preacher's hand before the preacher walked away.

You okay? he asked, refocusing Davina's attention as he steered her toward the cars parked near the curb. He pulled her into his arms and pressed a sweet kiss to her lips before smiling down at her. *You were a little distant back there. You haven't changed your mind, have you?*

Absolutely not. Davina kissed him back. *I love you, and I can't wait to be your wife. You promised me a do-over. Three boys and a house on the hill across the country from your parents. I have to run and pick up your surprise and get my ring cleaned.*

He released her and opened her car door. *Go run your errands. I'll see you tonight.*

I promise I won't be long. She smiled up at him and slid behind the wheel, pulling my energy into the passenger seat.

A picture of my father's serious face flashed on the screen.

"Stay in the moment with Davina," Doc Stone whispered in my ear, championing my directions.

I refocused my energy back inside the car. We were traveling now down dirt roads through the forest on the outskirts of town. The surrounding trees all looked the same. I had no idea where we were or which way we'd come. Panicking, I turned in the seat to look out the back window and all around, knowing the brief reprieve of my father's image might have made me miss something important. The beeping of the heart rate monitor sped up.

"You're doing great, Cree. She's on Old Mill Road. Just keep watching," Doc Stone prodded, calming my anxiety.

The car stopped, but Davina didn't get out. Tears slid down her red blotchy face as her grip on the steering wheel turned white. *I can't do this.*

A cell phone rang, and she bypassed the one sticking out of her purse and opened the middle console. She pulled out what I assumed was a burner phone and answered the call. *Hello.*

I hated when they used phones and I couldn't hear the rest of the conversation. It skewed things unless the police could track the person who called. They might not even know about this phone.

I'm almost there. I'm five minutes from the cabin, just wait for me.

I know what to do. Five minutes, that's all I need.

A few head nods and a quick goodbye and she held the phone while putting the car back into gear. Her foot accelerated on the gas. Her body bobbed up and down as she hit every hole in the road.

She stopped again, only this time it was in the middle of a rickety bridge that didn't even look safe enough to walk over, much less drive. She got out of the car, and I appeared by her side. *I'm stronger than this. I should have just told him the truth. God, why didn't I tell him?* she whispered through her tears.

What could have gone so wrong that this woman would be standing on a bridge crying the day before her wedding?

Davina tossed the burner phone into the water. Her entire body shook with her sobs as she climbed up the rotted wooden railing. My hand flew to cover my mouth.

"Don't do it." My heart raced. I wanted to grab her and tell her that everything would be okay.

I have to tell him the truth. Davina stood at the top of the railing. Her entire body trembled barely supported by shaky legs. What seemed like an eternity passed as she stared at the gushing flow. She shook her head and swiped at the tears. *No.*

She squatted, grabbed the railing, and started to climb back down. I let out the breath I'd been holding.

Gunfire rang out through the trees. The force of the impact was quick, striking Davina in the back and sending her over the railing into the rock-strewn water below.

"I have to pull you, Cree. Your vitals are dropping."

"Not yet, I haven't seen who pulled the trigger," I whispered and watched as Davina went under the water with her arms flailing. She never came back up. I spun around, my gaze scanning the trees, waiting for the shooter to step out. Nothing, not even the sound of a broken branch.

Seconds later, my eyes flew open. The icy frost of my breath escaped my lips as Doc Stone and Charlotte hurried to add blankets to my freezing body. My entire body shivered uncontrollably as I curled up into a ball. It was one of the only side effects from using Insight we couldn't figure out how to control. The longer I used the machine, the more dangerous it became.

"That was too close, Cree," Doc Stone complained. "You can't stay under that long next time."

He was right. I knew he was. I'd just hoped to catch a glimpse of the killer's face.

"She didn't want to die." I tried to nod but couldn't control my shivers.

It was the last thing I remembered before I fell into my familiar deep sleep.

I awoke to sunlight coming in through the ballroom windows. Davina was staring at me. The image of her sad eyes would haunt me if I didn't help solve her case. She was a woman in love, a woman with secrets; much like me. I might not get the answers I needed, but I could damn sure help figure out who took away her choice to live.

I turned toward the ballroom doors. The entire room was empty now. The machines sat dark and turned off. Every one of Davina's witnesses were gone or lurking somewhere else in the house.

Tossing the covers off of me, I climbed out of my bed and followed the sound of voices to the kitchen.

"She should be up by now," Freddie grumbled.

"She's fine. For a guy who ran with the mob, you're acting like a mother hen," Faraday said.

"Someone has to, old man."

These two would bicker the rest of their lives while living under the same roof. Faraday on the side of the law, and Freddie not afraid to break a few if it meant getting stuff done.

"I just checked on her, but feel free to go look again." Faraday's annoyance returned. "I have to go into town and pull Davina's police file. So it looks like you get babysitting detail."

"I can assure you both that I don't need a babysitter."

"That's debatable," Faraday grumbled, sipping his cup of coffee.

I headed straight for the coffee pot and poured a fresh mug. The black gold promised a quick kick to get my blood pumping again.

"Faraday, what gives? You've been moping and cranky for an entire week." I took a long sip of my coffee.

Faraday let out an aggravated breath. "Every time you use Insight, I wait for you to pick my old case, and every time you choose a different one. I'm close to retirement, Cree. I'm running out of time to solve it."

I slowly lowered my cup. "I didn't know one of those cold cases were yours. Why didn't you just say so?"

His brows furrowed. "I didn't want to jump the line."

"Face it, Cree, the old man is too stubborn to ask for help."

"I carry a gun, Freddie," Faraday growled.

"So do I, but I'm not above asking for help when I need it."

"Okay, you two. Just stop. Faraday, next time I use Insight, I'd be glad to work on your case to see what we get."

He met my gaze. "You will?"

"Absolutely. You're my godfather. I want you to find peace, and if I can make it happen, I'll do everything in my power to see it happen."

The smell of bacon and eggs made my stomach rumble.

"I'm not her babysitter, Faraday. I'm her bodyguard," Freddie said, changing the subject while handing me a piece of his bacon.

"I don't need one of those either."

Faraday and Freddie exchanged a look as I bit off a piece of bacon.

"Don't worry, Cree. Whenever you're ready to re-enter society, I'll always have your back, even if I have to be stalkerish about it."

If re-entering society meant a late afternoon coffee at five with my best friend in the center of town, then that day was today, and I had no intention of letting Freddie shadow me, stalkerish or otherwise.

"One day I'm going to set up a stand in the middle of Times Square and offer free psychic readings complete with a crystal ball and tarot cards. Hell, I might even chant a spell or two to really give them something to gossip about."

Freddie chuckled. "I'll charge extra for breaking you out of the psych ward."

"I can afford it." I stole another piece of his bacon. "You don't charge me at all."

DEADLY VOWS

Chapter 3

"I should have listened to him," I grumbled, leaning my seat back to stare up at the stars. I'd dropped off my last batch of cupcakes at the coffee shop, and I'd stayed and enjoyed coffee with Charlotte. Time had slipped by while we had some much-needed girl time discussing the merits of my choices of men.

I'd even managed to sneak out of the house to make the trip into town alone. Somewhere between coffee and my way home, my tire had deflated. It didn't help it had a gash the size of a knife blade across the tread. The locals blamed me for a head mobster beating his charges when, in reality, he'd been innocent of that crime. It wasn't my fault that he hadn't been the one to commit the offense. It appeared the locals hadn't gotten the memo. They were clinging to the grudge like I was a pair of bell-bottom jeans in the back of my closet.

I had a ten-mile hike when the sun receded behind the horizon and the moon rose into the night sky. Of course, I was in the middle of cell service hell, without a cell tower in sight. I sighed. Someone would surely come along and find me soon, maybe. I glanced at my watch again and tapped the screen to get the minute hand ticking again. Perfect. I sighed. My current view of watching the stars in the night sky was a million times better than trying to walk ten miles in heels.

The silhouette of an apparition appeared in the tree line. Her white dress was dirty and torn. Grammy always told me not to stare. Staring invited them closer, and in one blink, this one was standing on top of my hood, and not only that. I knew exactly who she was.

"Calinda Sparks."

"One and the same," she answered, and with a snap of her fingers, her attire changed into a black evening gown she'd worn in the last movie she'd acted in. The clothes were fitting if not a tad theatrical.

This was the image I remembered. The one the newspapers had flashed when announcing to the public she'd died. I was only fifteen at the time, but the news had surely rocked my Grammy. Calinda Sparks was the equivalent of royalty in the U.S.

"You're early. I'm not working your case yet, but if you'd care to tell me who killed you and where you hid the diamond, you'd save me a lot of time." Sliding out of my Jeep, I climbed up on my hood to get a better look at her ghostly face.

"Do you have a dream?" she asked, momentarily confusing me. "I did, and it was beautiful. He promised to marry me, you know." Her smile fell into a frown.

I didn't need to ask who. The affair she'd had with the Prince of Wellington had been making headlines for years.

"Right now, my dream consists of not having to walk back to my house."

"Your chariot is on the way." She winked, and the smile returned to her face as she slowly fizzled out of sight.

The first cold, fat raindrop landed smack-dab in the middle of my forehead, almost like the last "screw you" from the locals. In any other car, it wouldn't have mattered. In my car, that wasn't the case. The top of my Jeep would remain dry since it was packed nice and neat in my shed.

Thunder rumbled, and lightning flashed in the distance. The coming rain wouldn't kill me, but the oncoming lightning just might. I could see it now. The town would rejoice and probably proclaim it as a national holiday.

"I won't melt," I screamed up into the sky, slipping my phone out of my pocket and holding it up higher in the sky. Still not a single bar.

The rain came down harder from the sky just as lights shined on me from down the road. An unfamiliar sports car slowed. The dark tinted windows hid the driver's identity. If this was knife-weilding-tire-slashing happy local, there was a good chance Freddie and Faraday would find my dead body on the side of the road.

The door opened, and an umbrella appeared seconds before I saw the face. West Archer rounded the car and stared up at me. "What are you doing, luv?"

"I was just talking to Calinda Sparks."

"Why don't you ask her who killed her and where the diamond is? It would save us both some time." He glanced slowly around as if looking to see if the actress was still near.

"I already did and she didn't answer, but next time she pops in, I'll try and pin her down," I answered seconds before my foot slipped and had me falling toward the mysterious man who'd once darkened my doorstep.

He released his umbrella, letting it fly in the wind, but he caught me in his arms. "You're dangerous."

"And you're getting wet. Care to give me a lift?"

"I thought that's what I was already doing."

"She said she sent a chariot." I smiled up into his dark green eyes. The flecks of yellow darkened as I let him carry me like a bride across a threshold to his car. Normally I'd be complaining I was a woman and knew how to walk, but I relaxed, letting him do all the heavy lifting. It wasn't an everyday occurrence that a man carried me in his arms.

He lowered me to my feet and stared intently into my eyes while the rain poured down on our heads. It would have been a romantic moment with the right partner. He was soo *not* that guy.

"I'm not Prince Charming."

"True, but I think you have more than plenty enough horses under that hood to get me home. Besides, I don't need a prince. I sort of have one." I blurted out. "Well, technically he moved away and doesn't live here anymore, but he'll come back...maybe. Well, technically he hasn't yet, but he said he would."

I was a babbling idiot. What the hell was wrong with me? West Archer didn't need to know my personal business. The less he knew, the better. *Keep it professional.*

"If he were truly your prince, he would have never left."

He opened the door, and I slid onto the seat, waiting for him to get in on the other side. "You're smooth. I can see it in your eyes and in your smile. I'm sure women everywhere watch you walk into a room. You and your sexy accent just swooping in and commanding attention. I don't need a savior or a prince. I could have walked…with the right shoes."

He gave me that sexy grin, the kind that promised the fun and games were just beginning. "Are the glass slippers pinching your toes?"

"Just my brain cells." I turned to look out the window and whipped my head back in his direction. "I was beginning to think you changed your mind about our super-secret project."

He glanced my way. "Sorry, I'm late. I had a funeral to attend."

"You really are Prince Charming, aren't you? You killed the wicked stepsisters. Because let me just tell you, I would have kicked those tramps to the ground and stepped on them with my pretty crystal shoes."

He tossed the car into gear and chuckled. "Sadly not the evil stepsisters, but someone just as sinister; a terrorist."

Chapter 4

I couldn't have possibly heard him right. He didn't strike me as a hitman for hire. I glanced at him again. His suit fit to perfection, high end. I could tell just by the fabric, not to mention the Rolex watch around his wrist. Surely the FBI didn't work with hitmen. Did they?

My mouth parted as I stared at him. Words escaped me, and that was a first.

"Relax, luv, he deserved to die."

"No... I mean, yeah, I'm sure some people deserve to die like pedophiles and serial killers, but you sound trigger-happy, and I don't mean that you're happy to see your horse."

"Trigger the Horse, is that an actual thing?" He chuckled. "You're unusual, Cree Blue."

"At least I'm not a gun-toting, trigger-happy, fake-Prince Charming-people-killer."

"If it helps, he was a really bad terrorist who's killed thousands and was about to do it again." West shrugged. "It was either him or me."

I turned my gaze to look out the window at the passing trees. Him or me. I'm not sure I could argue with that. I would have killed to save my own life too. I almost had, but still. I turned back to him once more. "And you attended his funeral? Did you kill his widow too?"

I just couldn't wrap my brain around what he was saying. It was straight out of a Bruce Willis movie, where a dozen bad men were killed and no one thinks twice about their families left behind. Well, I did, I thought twice. God forbid movies like that were real events and I came across that many pissed-off spirits all at once.

His eyes sparkled with mischief as he glanced my way. "Why would I kill his widow? She didn't do anything wrong, and besides, the mourners didn't know who I was."

"I'm not sure I do, either. Maybe this working together thing is a bad idea. I mean, no offense, but I don't generally work with James Bond-type spy people. Not that you're

James Bond, are you? Where's the flame-throwing, missile-shooting control panel?" I ran my hand over the dashboard, looking for secret hidden buttons.

"You have a very active imagination."

He had a point. Here I sat, wet from head to toe. The villagers had slashed my tire. I had members of both the police and the mob living under the same roof. Maybe I was the one that needed help.

"Are you staying in town? If you are, I wouldn't mention my name. They kind of hate me."

"I doubt that." West pulled beneath the iron gate of the Lady Blue Plantation and slowly drove up the drive. He parked just as lightning flashed, striking somewhere behind the house. The sonic boom made my heart momentarily freeze. Within seconds all of the lights inside the house flickered off.

"That can't be good." I yanked the handle and hurried out of the car, jogging up the porch stairs. I threw open the door to find Freddie using the light on his phone to maneuver around the office, opening blinds.

He glanced over his shoulder at me. "You're in trouble."

"What got hit?" I asked, pulling out my phone to use as a flashlight and heading to the kitchen, leaving Freddie and West to follow.

"Not sure. Faraday went down to the basement to check it out."

"Need any help, luv?" West asked from behind us.

I grabbed some of the emergency candles and a lighter out of the cupboards and lit a few. I tossed West the lighter and grabbed the closest lit candle. "You can light the rest of them while I check on Faraday."

I headed out of the room just as Freddie spoke. "She's been waiting for you."

The basement door stood open. The creepy dark stairwell had scared me as a kid. My Grammy used to say what scared her was the small steep steps. She'd always worried she'd take a tumble and there wouldn't be any sexy fireman around to help her get back up.

"Faraday, are you down there?" I called out as I slowly descended the stairs.

"Yeah."

I let out a relieved breath I'd been holding and spotted him in the corner kneeling beside *Insight*. "Looks like it fried Insight and the heart monitor."

"Daddy left schematics for Insight. I'm sure we'll find someone to fix it. The heart machine can be replaced, but you can't. Are you sure you're okay?"

"Fit as a fiddle."

I'd never understood that saying. Were fiddles really fit?

Faraday rose and stretched his back, cracking some of his old bones. "Why are you wet? I thought you were lying down with a headache."

I cringed. "Well…see, here's the thing."

"She snuck out and got stranded," Freddie answered, jogging down the stairs. "The Brit found her standing on top of her Jeep in the rain."

Faraday gave me that disapproving stare, the kind my dad had perfected the minute I started to crawl.

"Don't start. I wasn't investigating." Yet. "I was having coffee with Charlotte, and someone had to deliver the cupcakes."

The air in the basement was getting stuffier by the minute. "Let's go back upstairs."

"You two go ahead. I need to check the circuit breaker."

"Okay." I started jogging up the stairs and turned. "Do you mind if I take your truck? My Jeep got a flat, and I need to go put the top back on before everything is ruined and drive it back to the house."

Faraday slid the keys out of his pocket and tossed them through the air.

"Thanks." I jogged up the stairs to find West waiting at the top.

"Everything good?"

"Sure, come on, Archer, you're with me."

"Now wait a minute," Freddie said, resting his hand on my arm. "You've already been off running around in town."

"I'm just going to get my Jeep."

"Uh-huh. Why don't I go?"

"Because Faraday might need your help," I answered as if he should have already known the answer.

"I'm your bodyguard, not Mr. Fix-It."

Cree let out a long sigh. "Well, bodyguard, this house is known to get kind of hot and muggy, so if you can sleep in those conditions, knock yourself out. Go get the Jeep, and I'll try to figure out the difference between those silly screwdrivers when he asks for one."

"I'll guard her body." West winked.

"Funny man. Don't antagonize him. You aren't Prince Charming. You're more like the court jester who doesn't realize his jokes aren't funny," I said, grabbing his arm and pulling him to the door.

"If he's the jester, what does that make me?" I heard Freddie call out.

I'd have to think about that response. Freddie was a great guy, if not a tad bit scary with all of those tattoos, his bulky arms, and the mean-ass scowl he normally sported.

"Bodyguard?" West asked, jogging through the rain behind me into the barn.

"Well, in all fairness, he did save my life," I answered wiping the rain from my arms before grabbing the soft top for the Jeep.

West took it from me, and I gestured to the truck.

I grabbed one of the tires and rolled it in his direction.

He lifted it without a single hesitation like the pint of ice cream I ate last night. "Anything else?"

I climbed up into the bed of the truck and opened the tool box to find a jack and lug nut wrench inside. "That should do it."

I climbed out onto the bumper and jumped down. "I'll drive."

"Are you always this bossy?"

"Yes. I could blame it on my southern roots, but I think I was just born this way." I didn't even have to think about the answer. He'd realize it soon enough. No sense on denying it.

"Let me grab my umbrella." West said jogging back out into the rain and returning seconds later. He hopped in as I turned the ignition key. The old jalopy sputtered to life with a little shake.

"Either you're Marry Poppins with a magical umbrella that just reappears when you need one, or you're a little OCD driving around with more than one in your car."

"You'll find I'm prepared for many things." He winked.

I pulled out of the garage and headed back toward the long stretch of road. The silence between us lingered as I made it back to my Jeep and started putting on the soft top. The seats were going to take forever to dry out. The rest of my stuff inside was probably ruined. I'd brought this on myself. I knew better than to take the top off without checking the weather. The flat tire, well, that was another story. That could have been anyone while I'd been in the coffee shop.

West decided I was too fragile to fix my tire, so he insisted on doing that part. I stood over him with the umbrella while he fought the tight lug nuts holding the tire in place. Thirty feet in front of me was another ghost I recognized. Well, I knew she didn't want to die. Davina Richards was standing in the middle of the road. A car was shining the lights on her before plowing right through her spirit. She pointed down the dirt road. Her voice was crystal clear in my head. "You need to hurry, or it will be gone."

"What will be gone?" I asked, trying to urge her closer.

"What's that, luv?" West asked.

I handed him the umbrella and walked toward Davina when she didn't answer. "What will be gone?"

"Hurry," she said, pointing again.

West appeared by my side, shielding the rain from my head. "Who are you talking to?"

"Davina Richards and we have to go," I answered and jogged back to the truck, starting it as West climbed in the passenger seat.

"Where are we going?"

I shrugged. I had no idea where we were going or what we'd find. Davina was standing in the middle of the pavement and pointing down the dirt road. I turned Faraday's truck in that direction.

"Do you always do this?"

"Do what?" My fingers tightened on the steering wheel while maneuvering through the rain-filled pot holes.

"Chase ghosts."

"It depends. I wouldn't normally, but in this case, she's saying we need to hurry." West grabbed the handle over the door as I hit a larger hole. "Sorry."

Davina was standing off in the distance, pointing down another smaller dirt path in the woods. I turned and had to hit my brakes. No way was I going to be able to maneuver Faraday's truck through those tight branches. I threw it into park and hopped out. West was quick to follow, holding the umbrella over my head.

"Are you familiar with these woods?"

"Only enough to know we won't get cell service."

"Great."

I skidded to a stop when Davina reappeared. She was standing at the edge of an old rickety bridge pointing to something below.

I slid down the side of the embankment through the mud. My feet sunk down into the wet muck with each step. I moved closer to where Davina was standing and stepped over a log. I gasped at Davina's dead, lifeless body whose arms were still wrapped around the log.

I tossed West my phone. "Go back to the plantation and tell Faraday I found Davina and where I am. He'll know what to do."

"I'm not leaving you here," West argued.

"Go," I hollered. "I'm not sure how much longer we have until the water washes her away," I said, struggling to pull the log farther onto the shore. I was probably damaging evidence, but it was either that or have to convince the PD that she'd washed down the river.

"Do not move." West pegged me with his glare and tossed me the umbrella.

"Wouldn't dream of it." I chewed my lip as I watched him run off.

Chapter 5

I had good intentions to sit by the riverbank and wait patiently until help arrived. Right up until the point that Davina appeared again and started pointing farther into the forest.

"What about your body?" I asked.

She didn't answer, only gestured with her hand for me to follow her. I held on to the umbrella, ready to fight off wild animals, as I followed her farther in, stopping only occasionally to mark my way much like those imaginary Bigfoot creatures might. I picked up sticks and crossed them into little tepee-looking things as I followed her for about half a mile deeper into the wet, muddy green vegetation. "Are we getting close?"

Again no answer. She wasn't a chatty one, but she did stop and pointed toward a cabin hidden out of sight.

"Is this where you were going that day?"

Davina vanished out of sight as I approached the cabin and peeked through the dirt-caked windows. No one appeared to be home, but I knocked anyway. The last thing I needed was some squatter pulling a gun on me. With my second knock, the door pushed open. Okay, so maybe after I turned the handle, but regardless, it opened. No one needed to be the wiser.

"Hello?" I called out and peeked inside with the point of the umbrella leading the way.

A bed with mussed sheets sat in the corner. The smell of mildew lingered in the air as I moved inside. Plates sat in the sink with mould growing around the rims. Candles sat on the table, the wax long dried after running down the side. The place seemed usable but unoccupied like the owner hadn't been around in months.

A feeling of safety settled into my bones. Whoever lived here had felt safe being tucked away in the woods. I wasn't so optimistic.

I pulled open the bedside drawers, looking for anything that might tell me who called this place home. Several of the drawers were empty. I moved to the dresser by the bed and opened the top drawer. A picture of Davina and a man rested on top. His identity was blacked out with a marker. I flipped it over, to find nothing written on the back.

Beneath that were clothes. I pulled out a pair of jeans and unravelled them. They were Davina's petite size. I refolded them and shoved them back inside before closing the top drawer and moving to the next one. The second drawer had more clothes inside, only these were kind of dressy.

I shut the drawers and glanced around the room, turning back to the bed. In my younger days, I'd hidden a diary under my bed. I lifted the mattress to find Davina hadn't been like me. I'd turned to check the other side of the room when my foot snagged on a black handle. I pulled the backpack out and unzipped it. Sitting inside were wrapped hundred dollar bills. I flipped through them to find they were in sequential order.

I put them back and unzipped another compartment. In that one, I found an invitation addressed to Davina for an exclusive one-week charity event being held by Senator Preston Channing and his family at an island resort they owned and it was scheduled for tomorrow.

"Interesting." I shoved the invite back down into the bag and unzipped the next compartment and found a single note. *You know what to do.*

I unzipped the outside compartment. Several IDs sat inside. They all had Davina's pictures but with different names.

I sighed and slipped the backpack over my shoulder, refusing to leave that kind of money in Davina's cabin for some crazy swamp man to come along and steal. I walked out of the cabin and headed back to Davina's remains, using my bread crumbs of twigs.

"Cree." I heard Faraday hollering.

I followed the voice.

"I told her to stay." West Archer's voice carried.

"You don't know her well if you think just telling her to stay would actually work. That's why I should have been the one to come with her," Freddie argued back.

"Easy, boys," I said, stepping out of the trees. "I'm fine, and I wouldn't have listened to either of you."

The police and forensic people were standing around the body while others were figuring a way to stop the water from washing away any more of their evidence. It was a losing battle. Mother Nature was finicky that way.

The chief lingered on the bridge, staring down at all of us. Rain slid in a constant stream from the wide brim of his police-issued hat.

I waved and tried to climb back up through the mud slush. With each step, my foot sunk a little farther into the sludge. I only got stuck once until a hand landed on my butt, giving me a shove.

I glanced over my shoulder to find West's gaze right on my rear. "I may not be a prince, but chivalry isn't dead."

I rolled my eyes as I made it up to the bridge trying to shake the fresh wet mud from my jeans. I headed straight for the chief.

People were funny when they saw me coming. Some pretended not to even notice me, and others went out of their way to avoid me. The chief, well, when he saw me coming, he knew that death had reared its big ugly head and his department was about to earn their paychecks.

I handed him the backpack. "That belonged to Davina Richards. You'll find she was shot in the back while standing on a bridge similar to this one. She fell over, and poor thing couldn't swim. I'm sure the water carried her down this way."

"This is the cold case you were working?"

"Yep." I sighed. "There's a cabin about a half-mile in the woods. She appeared to either be living there or staying there. This is her bag."

"Did you look inside?"

Duh. Of course, I had. "You might want to start with figuring out Davina's real identity. She has several IDs in that bag with different names and addresses."

"IDs?"

"Several," I answered.

The chief started unzipping the bag and paused at the cash.

"Those sequential bills may offer you a clue."

"Are you getting any vibes?"

That was a good question. Strangely I wasn't getting any vibes. Normally that kind of money would carry a ton of emotional energy, but I wasn't picking up on anything. "Not really, but I did snoop through her drawers, so you'll find some of my fingerprints in the cabin."

He zipped the backpack and pegged me with his glare. "How did you find the cabin?"

"Davina pointed the way. I may be crazy, but trampling around in the woods in the rain just for the hell of it is more than my brand of nuts. I don't even like to camp." I shivered and rubbed my arms. "If it's okay with you, I'd like to go change out of these wet clothes."

The chief nodded. "If I have more questions, I'll drive out to the Plantation."

I spun to leave and then stopped. "I need a favor."

"What's that?"

"Check surveillance around the coffee shop and find out who slashed my tire."

He nodded. "Do you want to press charges?"

"Heck no." I grinned. "I want to return some of the love and joy they gifted me." I tried to say it like I meant it, complete with a smile on my face. I really did.

"Ms. Blue." He used his authoritative tone, the one that made criminals wince in the kind of way that if my tire slasher happened to show up dead, I'd be the first suspect.

"Being stranded on a deserted road with no cell service kinda sucked. I couldn't even play games on my phone to pass the time. Where's the justice in that?" I started walking backward. "Oh yeah, I'm not sure you'll find it, but right before she was shot, she threw a cell phone into the water."

"Her phone was in the car," he said.

"Not that phone." I grinned. "And she got a call before she tossed it."

West walked with me back toward the road where my poor Jeep was still sitting. "How could you possibly know she tossed a phone in the water?"

"There's a lot you don't know about me, Mr. Spy Guy." I looked his way as if he were a lifetime rider of the short bus and not the super-secret agent who had killed a terrorist.

"I look forward to finding out all your secrets, Lady Blue," he said, handing me the keys and jumping into the passenger side of the Jeep.

When he sat, the water from inside the seats pushed to the top from his weight. He cringed but only slightly. I handed him back the umbrella.

"Thanks for leaving me your weapon."

He chuckled. "You have no idea." He waited until I got behind the wheel when he pulled at the handle of the umbrella to show a long thin sword hidden inside the shaft.

"Well, that's nifty. Was that a graduation present from spy school?"

"It was a present from my mother."

"Mine gave me pearls when I turned sixteen. I think she believed I'd grow up to be a proper southern lady."

"Didn't you?"

"Not even close but I'm a fabulous drama queen." I turned the engine and revved the gas. Every cop I knew was working down near the river. I laid my foot on the gas driving the way my Grammy taught me all those years ago.

West remained suspiciously quiet as I drove back to the Plantation. Maybe it was the cold rainwater seeping through the seat freezing his family jewels or he'd finally realized that we wouldn't work well together since I wasn't the type that followed directions. "Why are you so quiet? Are you trying to find a polite way to tell me we can't work together?"

He rubbed his chin as I pulled under the iron gate. "On the contrary, I'm trying to figure out what it's going to take to get you to focus on my case."

I killed the ignition and shoved my door open. "That's an easy answer. I need to solve this case, and then I'm all yours."

"All mine, huh? The fed really is gone." He got out of the Jeep and followed me up the steps and into the stuffy house.

The working lights were a pleasant surprise. Not that I was afraid of the dark or the things that went bump in it. Just the opposite. I grew up hearing strange noises and unexplainable creaks. Disappearing into the laundry room, I grabbed some clean towels and handed him one while I wrung out the water in my hair. "You asked for my focus, nothing else, Jester."

He chuckled. "Fair enough. How can I help you figure out this case?"

I swiped the towel over my face. "I don't suppose you have a matching invite like the one I found in Davina's bag. It was to an exclusive island charity event sponsored by Senator Preston Channing."

"Not yet," he said and slipped his keys out of his pocket and turned to leave, stopping at the door. "Have breakfast with me at the Reliance Hotel."

"Oh, now see, you don't know me very well. I'm the worst morning person, ever. I'm more of an anti-morning person. I'm worse than the ugly green witch in *The Wizard of Oz* and more ornery than if she and Attila the Hun were to have kids. I'd be just like one of them if I have to get up before eight a.m. without an IV drip of hot coffee oozing into my veins. It's rumored I'm like a rabid dog that goes for the jugular when people try to wake me up."

His lips twisted into a smile. "I can't wait to experience it first-hand. What if I promise copious amounts of caffeine and a present? I'll even be very quiet until you're normal again."

"On one condition."

"Name it."

"You'll show me where all the secret gadgets are in your car so if we're being chased I can blow something up."

"Unfortunately this car isn't equipped with toys for you to play with, but I promise after, when we work on Calinda's case, I'll have my other one brought over and waiting for us in California."

I was quiet as if debating an answer when I was really waiting to see if there was some delay in my lie detector. It hadn't gone off since he arrived.

"Lie to me."

"Excuse me?"

"Tell me a lie and make it a big honking whopper that would get you in trouble."

"You're ugly."

Liar flashed in neon red letters in my mind, but it might have been just my ego correcting his words.

"That's subjective. Tell me another lie, but not about me."

"Are you sure you didn't fall and hit your head?"

"Quit being a pansy and lie like your life depends on it." I raised my brow in challenge.

"The fed is a smart man for leaving you."

Liar flashed again.

"Really?"

"No, Cree. Not really. Lucky for me, he made a huge mistake."

Goosebumps rose on my arms, giving me my own personal sign that he was telling the truth. West really believed his words. "Fine, lots and lots of coffee at eight a.m., but don't say I didn't warn you that I'll be grumpy."

"Duly noted," he said, and without a single look back, he walked out the door and took my towel with him. The thief.

DEADLY VOWS

Chapter 6

―――――――◗◉◖―――――――

West held the phone to his ear as the waitress brought him a third cup of coffee. Her cheeks had turned a pretty shade of pink as she smiled at him. Any other time he'd ask for her number, but the only color he had on his mind was Blue. Cree Blue to be more exact.

"West, are you even listening to me?" Phillip asked.

Phillip Wellington, the Prince of Wellington, hated to be ignored. His last name alone commanded attention, most of the time. It was of no surprise his ancestors had named the entire kingdom after themselves. West would know. He'd grown up ignoring orders from his best friend his entire life. "I hear you, Phillip."

"What is taking so long? Why isn't the American making this her top priority?" Annoyance slipped into Phillips' voice. They both knew the importance of finding the diamond and the reason it needed to be returned.

"She isn't just some woman who can be ordered around. She has a good heart, and helping people is what she does."

"Offer her money to make it her priority. Do whatever needs to be done to make it happen."

"She won't take it," West argued. He might not know Cree well, but he knew her well enough from the background check he'd done on her to know that money wouldn't be a motivator. She didn't accept payments on the cases she helped solve. "She's working a case, and once it's solved, she promised to concentrate on Calinda and the diamond."

"She's chasing criminals? Is she a private investigator or a cop? Can she even defend herself? What if she dies before getting to *my* case?"

"She's a baker."

The line went silent. West loved screwing with Phillip, and he could only imagine how red his face was getting.

Cree walked in the door, her face set in a frown. West snapped his fingers, and a waitress greeted her at the door with a cup of Cree's favorite coffee, and another waitress appeared with two more, setting them on the table in front of the empty chair.

Cree sipped and continued sipping until she sat plopped down into the seat. Her eyes closed, and she moaned her approval.

"West, offer her the money."

He shook my head. "You do it."

West handed the phone to Cree and grinned as she lowered her coffee cup. Her eyes narrowed to slits. "I warned you."

"I know." He tried to hide his grin and failed. "This should be fun."

Cree took the phone and held it to her ear. "What?"

He couldn't hear Phillip, but West could imagine how the conversation was going, just by the slow rise of Cree's brow. "No."

There was a slight pause. "Thor could ask while shirtless and swinging his hammer with Magic Mike as his backup dancer and I'd tell him the same thing; the answer is still no."

She ended the call by hitting the off button and slid the phone across the table before picking up the second cup of coffee. West picked up his coffee, and waited patiently until she was ready to start her day.

It took only three cups of coffee and an assortment of pastries before life returned to her eyes. "The Prince of Wellington offered me an insane amount of money to drop my case."

"I'm sure he did. I'd apologized for him, but I'd already told him you wouldn't bite. He didn't believe me."

"I hung up on him," Cree said, taking a sip of her fourth cup of coffee.

"I noticed." West grinned and took a sip of coffee.

"I probably started an international incident."

"I'm sure you'll always remain memorable." West chuckled. "So, Cree, good morning."

Cree smiled in that charming way that tiptoed the line from devious serial killer to almost human. "You promised me a surprise. I hope that the phone call wasn't what you had planned."

"Give me more credit than that. I not only have one surprise, I have two."

"Two?" she asked picking up a piece of bacon from his plate and taking a bite.

"Would you like me to order you some bacon, first?"

"No, yours is fine."

West pulled the envelope out of his jacket and slid it across the table to her, not releasing it until she met his gaze. "I have a condition of my own."

Cree sat back in her chair with a harrumph. "What is it?"

"We do this together or not at all."

Cree rose from her seat. "I don't take orders well, especially at this time of the morning."

"Sorry, luv, this is non-negotiable. That invitation is addressed to me."

Her gaze went back to the envelope. "You got an invitation to the exclusive event?"

He nodded and gestured for her to sit. She plopped back down into her chair like a child made to return to the table to eat her broccoli. "The condition is that you'll need to be my plus one."

She peeked inside the envelope. A slow smile formed on her lips. "I can do plus one."

"The festivities end with a formal ball, so you'll need the attire."

"Oh." She glanced up at him. "I have the perfect dress."

"We'll need to be discreet with our snooping and minimize the number of toes we step on."

"I can be discreet."

He doubted that. Cree wasn't the type of woman who would blend in. She was the kind of beautiful that any man worth a damn would notice. West lifted the paper he'd been reading before she arrived and slid a copy of the file beneath it across the table. It was a copy of the complete Billson PD file they'd compiled on Davina's case.

She flipped it open before lifting her gaze to his. "Where did you get this?"

"I have my ways. I figured we could solve it faster if we weren't starting from scratch."

"This is perfect." She lowered her gaze back down again, and he sat patiently while she read the entire file. "Her fiancé was the senator's son?"

"You must not watch the news a lot. I'm sure it made headlines for days."

"I avoid the news as much as possible, too much death and crime. All it takes is one look at a face of someone missing or dead and I tune in like a mosquito looking for a fresh blood supply. I have a hard time letting those cases go and let's be honest; not everyone believes clues that come from a psychic."

"I can't say I'd watch too much TV either, if I were you." He gestured to the file. "Looks like they had a short engagement."

She closed the file. A frown marred her face. "They haven't finished the autopsy or noted any fingerprints in the cabin."

"It's been less than a day, Cree. They aren't miracle workers. Give them time. Deputy Director Harrison Reed will give us updates."

Her frown slowly slid into a smile at the mention of Harrison's name. A twinkle filled her bright blue eyes. West silently wondered what it would take to get that same twinkle hearing his name instead. "How is Harrison these days?"

Harrison Reed had been the man to send West to Cree a month ago after she sent him an anonymous warning letter about his daughter's run-in with a stalking serial killer. If it hadn't been for Cree's warning, there was no telling how many more victims the killer would have claimed.

"The deputy director is still very thankful, and he'll also be a guest on the Island. He said you might need backup considering you constantly find yourself in trouble."

"And here I thought I was the drama queen. I had that last situation all under control." Cree dismissively waved her hand.

"Well, it won't hurt to have him and a few of his agents on the Island knowing what you're up to."

"It's unnecessary. I'd hate to put him out and make him come all this way."

"Senator Channing and Harrison are friends. He was already planning to attend."

"Friends in high places must be convenient," she grumbled as if all the joy had been sucked from her body and replaced with something sour.

West handed her another piece of bacon. "Harrison is a fair man, Cree. He's looking forward to meeting you."

West rose from his seat and slipped some bills on the table to pay the tab. "You should go home and pack. I'll swing by and pick you up in about an hour after I run a couple of errands. That should give you plenty of time to break it to your bodyguard that he has to sit this one out."

Cree rose while tipping her cup back to savor the last of the coffee. She grabbed the last piece of bacon and pointed it at me. "Freddie isn't going to like that. Do you mind if I hold on to the file?"

"Not at all." West walked her to the door and out into the lobby. "I'll see you in an hour."

Cree didn't even glance back as she left the hotel. She wasn't what he would call very observant of her surroundings. Businessmen were watching her walk out, along with a few of the bellboys. West took a seat and waited to see if any of them would follow her. He might be paranoid, but paranoia had kept him alive all these years and was the only thing that saved his best friend's life and everyone in the castle when West stopped the terrorist. It paid in his line of work to be cautious. Speaking of which, more backup on a reclusive island might not be a bad idea. West slid the phone out of his suit pocket and dialed Cree's home number.

"Blue residence," Freddie answered on the first ring.

"Freddie, this is West Archer. Can you meet me at the Reliance Hotel Room 310? It's concerning Cree."

"I'll be there in fifteen minutes."

"Excellent."

****

West was shoving his gun into the waistband of his suit when someone knocked on the hotel door. After pressing his eye to the peep hole, he unlocked it and pulled it open. "Thanks for coming."

"Always for Cree," Freddie said, following West into the room. "What's going on?"

Freddie stiffened as his gaze traveled around the room. West had guns sitting next to the open half-packed suitcase on the bed. Surveillance equipment and other gadgets sat out on the desk. "Cree is on the hunt for Davina's killer, and we're going to an Island where I'm guessing most of the suspects will be."

"You can go, but she's not walking into danger without me having her back." Freddie crossed his arms.

His scowl would intimidate most men, but it had little effect on West's intentions. "That's why you're here. There are several feds that will be in attendance, but I need someone invisible monitoring her every move. Her safety is my priority and something I won't leave up to chance."

"I'm listening." Freddie dropped his arms.

West grabbed the rolled picture from the closet and unrolled it, using a gun to hold it down. "This is a satellite image of the island that I got this morning."

He'd had to call in favors for some quick surveillance and intel on what they were walking into. He'd never gone blind into any mission, and he wasn't about to start now, no matter how headstrong Cree was.

"I've got enough bugs to cover most of the area, including a tracker that I'm going to plant on Cree, so there won't be any place she goes that you won't be able to find her."

"You aren't going to tell her, are you? She's going to be pissed if she finds out."

"Pissed is better than dead, don't you agree?"

He sighed and glanced at the map again. "Personally, I think she's come a long way since I saved her life. She's stronger, she can shoot a gun, and I've been teaching her defensive techniques to get out of any jam, but you're right. I'd feel better if I was there."

"Excellent." West pointed to the map. "That's why I'll have a boat at the marina, ready to take you across to the island to this cabin. I already set up everything you're going to need to monitor the situation. I'll have a tracker on both her and me. You'll be able to tell if she decides to go running off and chasing bad guys without me."

"Who the hell are you?" Freddie asked as he walked over to the table and picked up some of the gadgets. "Your gadgets are more expensive than even the military or government agencies use. You aren't the mob; they wouldn't be this organized. They tend to shoot first and ask questions later." Freddie gestured to the map. "You obviously have some big contacts, and you're running this like a well-planned mission."

"Let's just say I have the backing of an entire country to see that she comes out of this unscathed and lives to work on a case that is severely more important."

Freddie tossed the gadgets on the desk. "And when that's done? Will she come out unscathed from that one, and after dealing with you?"

"I'm not the fed that broke her heart. I haven't promised anything that I can't deliver."

"See that you don't," Freddie threatened. "You might have the weight of a country backing you, but I have the mob. She got

Moreno, the head boss, out of a jam, and he's taken an interest in watching out for her. He's got her back, and he's much more ruthless, cunning, and patient than you can ever imagine, so if you don't want to continuously be looking over your shoulder, you won't fuck with her. Are we clear?"

"You're threatening me?"

He shook his head. "That's not a threat; that's a promise."

"Good answer. We both have the same goal." West moved back to the map, going over exactly what he was going to need Freddie to do.

Chapter 7

The island was stunning from a bird's-eye view. I'd been hesitant to climb into the helicopter with West, but the view alone was worth the ride, even if my stomach disagreed. The flight to the exclusive resort was short and sweet over roads with unbelievable views of waterfalls and greenery. The huge mansion resort was everything I'd thought it to be. Fit for a senator and all of his friends, who probably tossed money around the way I included ingredients in my most-sought-after desserts.

Men in suits were stationed at the resort doors as we entered.

"There are a lot of political and famous people attending," West whispered in my ear.

His hand was splayed on my lower back as he guided me toward the reception area. I didn't know where to look first. Chandeliers hung from the painted ceilings. Expensive Italian marble covered the floors. Everything about this place screamed affluence, and I was more worried than the mother of a toddler that my shoes would scuff the floors.

"Welcome to Killington." The woman smiled first at West and then at me. "Name please."

"West Archer," he answered, and then the woman looked at me.

"I'm his plus one." I pointed my thumb in his direction.

Her fingers clicked over the keyboard. "I'm sorry, but I don't have a West Archer on the guest list." She glanced at me. "Or his plus one."

"Well, you wouldn't; he's too modest." An older gentleman walked over to us and held out his hand to West. "His official name is Lord West Archer attending on behalf of Prince Wellington with full authority to handle the King and Prince's affairs."

"Get out." I nudged West's arm. "And here I thought you were the jester."

"Ah yes, we have your first name listed as Lord Archer, my apologies. Can I have the name of your guest, Lord Archer?"

The older gentleman took both my hands in his. "This woman is so much more than anybody's plus one. She, my dear, is Cree Blue of the Lady Blue Plantation, who was personally sponsored by me and my daughter."

I glanced from suit man to West and back. "Harry?"

He chuckled. "Deputy Director Harrison Reed," he corrected.

"Harry," I exclaimed louder and pulled the old man in for a hug. My actions caught everyone off guard, and a few of the suits nearby looked ready to pounce until Harrison held up his hand, staying their movement. "How's Glynis? Did you assign Frick and Frack this detail?"

I glanced around, really taking a look at the suits surrounding me to see if Agents Hunter and Fernandez, whom I'd met a month ago, were among the faces. They weren't, but there was one face I recognized staring back at me. I'd recognize those baby blue eyes and that menacing scowl anywhere. They belonged to my almost-boyfriend, who had been avoiding me like the plague. Newly appointed FBI Agent Leonard Mason Spencer.

My smile and joy from seconds ago momentarily slipped as Mason's gaze went to where West had his hand nestled on my back.

"Are you referring to the two agents I sent to find you a month ago?"

"Of course." She grinned.

"Ah, well, Frick and Frack weren't available, but my daughter is great. She's here, and she's dying to meet you at the cocktail reception this evening." Harry said, pulling my attention back to him.

"I'm looking forward to it," I said, trying to keep the questions from my face.

"Lord Archer. Here are your keys. I'll have the concierge take you to your cabana."

"We aren't staying in the resort hotel?" I asked, glancing up at West.

"I thought you might like some privacy to get some work done," he said, smiling down at me.

"Sure." Because that was what every woman would do on a secluded island surrounded by millionaires with a beach less than fifty yards away. Work. Was that what I had succumbed to, a woman so focused on helping solve cold cases that I didn't even enjoy my surroundings? My Grammy was right. I was going to die a lonely old cat lady, only without any cats and only ghosts to keep me company. Maybe I'd pick some place like this to haunt in my demise. Pity party for one; I could almost hear Charlotte and Freddie's voice in my head telling me to snap out of it.

"Lord Archer, Ms. Blue, if you'll just follow me," the concierge said, sliding my bag off my shoulder and slipping my suitcase from my hands.

I couldn't help but hold Mason's gaze as we passed. Sucked I wasn't a mind reader to know what was going on in that big head of his. There was a conversation in my future, and it had the makings to become ugly.

"Stop frowning, luv," West whispered in my ear as we walked out of the lobby. "You're ruining our charade."

"Lord?" That one word had the ability to make his noble highness stop telling me what to do.

I had a job to do, one that I was more determined than ever to make happen and fast. I needed to start with the fiancé or those closest to him. I wasn't here to make friends or play nice with the feds. Gah. I needed to bake. I needed to get my head on straight.

We arrived at the cabana, and West tipped the concierge as I took my bags into the bedroom and dropped them, opening all the other doors. The cabana was exactly like I'd thought it would be. The natural light coming in through the windows and sheer curtains made it a tiny oasis with views of the sugar-white sandy beach. I returned to the living room.

"There's only one bedroom, and I'm not sleeping with you."

"Relax, Cree. I'll take the couch. You can have the room."

I should have protested and offered to sleep on the couch, but I was no longer in the mood to play nice.

I walked back into the bedroom and hung up the dresses that I'd brought and unpacked my clothes. I was standing at the window looking out into the ocean when I heard West enter the room behind me.

"I have a title, but it doesn't define who I am."

"Oh, I know." I was a pretty good judge of character and with digging up the truth unless it came to picking boyfriends. "You're West Archer. You're just helping me so I can move on to your case."

"Cree..."

I shook my head and unfolded my arms. I grabbed my swimsuit and headed for the bathroom. "We're good; all I ask is that you just don't lie to me even if I don't like your answer."

"Fair enough. If you ask, I'll be honest."

I spun at the door to the bathroom and pointed at him. "See, that's the thing. You don't think I'm smart enough to ask the right questions, so you won't have to answer, but you're wrong."

"I'd never underestimate you, Lady Blue."

A slow smile filled my lips as I lifted the hem of my dress slowly up my thigh. I pulled the Velcro strap holding the knife and sheath from around my thigh and tossed them onto the bed. I walked over to my suitcase and pulled out an identical invite and tossed that on top. The invite didn't have his name scrolled over the top; it had mine. Next, I pulled out the picture that I'd printed three weeks ago from the internet. It had taken a full day of searching for Charlotte, Jitters, and I to find it, but it was one of him and his best friend, the prince, dressed in polo player attire with their titles and names beneath. I tossed the picture next to the invite. "You already have, Lord Archer."

"Damn it. I missed deleting that one."

After changing into my bathing suit and wrapping a sarong around my body, I put on a big floppy hat. I looked like a million bucks. How did I know? I might have had a dead actress help me pick it out while I spent the entire time trying to convince her to tell me who killed her and where the diamond was hidden. Trying to pin down her answers was the equivalent of using a knife as a fly swatter. Every time I asked, she managed to flitter on about something else.

When I walked out into the living room, West had the phone pressed to his ear as he turned around. His mouth parted as his gaze slid down my body and back up.

He visibly swallowed. "Wow."

I winked. "I can play any role. Drama major, remember?"

"Do you want company?" he asked then said, "No, not you, Phillip. I'm talking to Cree."

"I'm following my gut. Where better to find out all gossip then straight into the middle of the hen house. Women like to brag about all kinds of things, and I'm sure there are plenty of drunken women with loose lips sitting by the pool. If that doesn't work, then I'll make friends with the men or the staff. I haven't decided which next."

West

Chapter 8

"Tell me when she leaves the room so I can have your attention again." Phillip's aggravated tone poked West's nerve.

"She was wearing a bikini," he said, as if that would explain his lack of attention on him.

"You've seen plenty of women dressed in less than that, West. I'm beginning to question if you'll be able to do the right thing when all of this is over. You realize what's at stake."

"I've always done my duty for your family and our country." Anger swept through his body as he entered the bathroom and picked up Cree's watch sitting on the counter. "Listen, I've got to go. My time alone in this room is limited and I need to work my magic and keep her alive."

"West, Katherine and I worry about you."

"I know," West answered. Phillip and his wife, Katherine, and West had been thick as thieves growing up. It had been him who tried to talk sense into Phillip when he started the affair with the actress. He'd been young then, cocky, and wasn't interested in becoming a monarch. If it wasn't for Calinda Sparks' death and getting his own priorities straight, there was no telling where Phillip might have ended up; definitely not trusted with the crown. The clock was ticking for West to fix things for good. This island was the last place he needed to be. The quicker he could get Cree off of it, the more time they'd have to save what mattered most; his country's legacy.

"Katherine and Elizabeth are best friends. They tell each other everything, and Elizabeth said you haven't returned her calls in two weeks."

West sighed and clenched his eyes closed. Elizabeth was the last thing he wanted to discuss with his best friend. West didn't care how close his wife was to his ex-girlfriend. He was trying to keep Katherine and Phillip out of his personal life. "She cheated on me, and we broke up. I've already moved on."

Silence momentarily filled the line. "It's the American, isn't it?"

"Did you hear a word I just said, Phillip? She cheated on me. We're done. End of discussion. Now if you'll let me get back to work, I'm busy here, saving Cree's ass so she can save yours."

"I don't like your tone," Phillip announced.

"I don't like you prying. Give Katherine my love and break the news to her that I don't need her to set me up with any more of her friends. Lie to her if you must and tell her I've fallen for a beautiful, psychic, baker from America. That will give her and Elizabeth plenty to discuss."

"You haven't, have you?" Phillip asked, his tone turned serious.

"I'm working. Goodbye, Phillip. Give your mother and father my best and tell them I'll be back soon."

He hung up on Phillip, much the way Cree had early that morning. West tossed his phone onto the bed and unzipped the bag, pulling out a slim piece from his lock kit to pry the back of Cree's watch open. He pulled out the battery and replaced it with the one that had the GPS locator attached before pushing the backing back into place. West put the watch back exactly as she had it and went about setting up all of the other gadgets in the room.

When he was happy, he picked up the phone and dialed Freddie. "Are you picking up the signal?"

"It's showing in the cabana area with both your GPS and hers, and you're positioned a half-mile from my location."

"Perfect. I placed it in her watch, and she's at the pool, so I'm heading there now. The cocktail party is in two hours. Call my cell if the signals separate."

"Of course."

"I'll keep you posted on the location of the other bugs I plant in the hotel. Let me know if you need reinforcements to help monitor."

"No need. I brought my own."

His words made West pause. "Who?"

"Jitters and a few other techies I trust who are just as determined to watch her back."

"That wasn't the plan," West growled, sliding out of the suit jacket.

"It wasn't *your* plan, but it was mine. More eyes on the prize. I'll text you if we spot trouble."

Chapter 9

I sauntered into the pool area and straight up to the bar. Calinda had appeared by my side on the walk to the pool. *Be confident, chin up, and if they show their claws, you show yours. They'll think twice about attacking the guest of a lord. They'll cling to you because knowing you will make them appear more important.*

I was taking the advice of a ghost, granted a beautiful movie star ghost, but a dead woman nonetheless. I slid onto one of the bar stools at the end of the bar and ordered a glass of wine. Thanks to Calinda, I knew just the right year to make the impression I intended.

Two women sat nearby, and another one sat alone at the other end.

One of the two next to me glanced my way, and I tried for a sugary-sweet smile. Neither looked ready to play nice. Both women wore bikinis. The older woman had a diamond necklace around her scrawny neck. Their nails were painted in a French manicure, and each woman looked like they'd spent an eternity in the gym. All nice, tan arm candy for these men.

"This is a lovely little getaway."

They smiled in a way that they appeared ready to stab me in my eye and steal my dessert. I ignored them both and inhaled a deep breath of fresh ocean air. The sun hung high in the sky, and the views were outrageously great. No way would I let these women ruin my mood. They weren't drunk enough to give me the answers I'd came to find.

"You can charge it to my cabana. I'm in suite 2 with Lord Archer."

The women at the bar exchanged a look. Scrawny-neck lady slid the glasses off her eyes to rest on her head. "I don't believe we've met. I'm Priscilla."

I knew her name. I'd done a workup after being given Davina's case file and being caught off guard that Davina was engaged to the senator's son, Logan. Scrawny-neck lady was Priscilla Channing, the groom's mom. I could even identify the woman sitting next to her. I'd read their alibis.

"You're Senator Channing's wife. It's a pleasure to meet you."

"This is Clarissa Jones, she and my son, Logan, are lifelong friends and business partners."

"Oh dear. I was sorry to hear about Logan's fiancée. I'm sure her death was devastating and so close to the wedding. I ran into Davina that morning, and she told me that she and Logan were going to the chapel one last time." I lied like a room full of politicians on Election Day.

Clarissa eyed me like I'd just peed in the pool. "You were friends with Davina?"

"We both enjoyed frequenting Millie's Roast, the coffee shop downtown. That's where we met. Sweet girl, but kind of quiet." I hoped. As a ghost, she didn't have much to say, anyway.

"She didn't drink coffee." Clarissa tapped her claws on the bar.

"They serve more than coffee. You should try their pastries."

"Oh I just love their specialty white chocolate cupcake with...what does that have on it?" Priscilla asked.

"Cashews," I answered. I should know; I created it. "It's one of my most-sought-after creations. They can't keep those cupcakes in the shop for an hour before they get sold out."

"You're Cree Blue? The baker? I've eaten a slice of one of your wedding cakes, and I swear I gained ten pounds that day, but it was so worth it. Every bite was better than the last." Clarissa's mouth parted.

"You've tasted my sweets." I sounded so naughty. "I'm always happy to hear when others enjoy my desserts as much as I enjoyed baking them."

"I'd love to get your card and have you make my wedding cake if that time ever comes."

"It will dear, trust me." Priscilla patted her hand before turning her glare onto me, smacking me in the face with her mood swing. "You're that psychic responsible for freeing that despicable mob boss, Moreno."

"Actually he was accused of killing someone who wasn't dead. Who knew?"

"You should have let him rot in jail," she grumbled.

"That seems to be the consensus." I had a slashed tire to prove it.

"It's hard to believe that you're friends with a lord," Priscilla said, lowering her glasses over her eyes, dismissing me as a worthy conversationalist and taking another long sip of her whisky on the rocks.

I hid my smile with the perverse knowledge that my high-calorie cupcakes constantly sent this woman to the gym. I'd have to send her a dozen when this was over as a special "screw you," maybe complete with a cake too.

A woman from the end of the bar picked up her glass of wine and moved into the seat next to me. "Be nice, Priscilla. Cree means well. She saved my life."

I turned to the woman, and it was only then I noticed she had the same brown eyes as Deputy Director Harrison Reed.

"Glynis?"

"In the flesh, thanks to you." She clinked her glass with mine. "Cree is the whole reason I cleared my schedule to attend with dad. She's a celebrity; she just doesn't realize it yet. She's getting a commendation from the president himself, and she was first on my list to be invited to the White House for my wedding."

"Wait, what?" I turned to her, and that was when I realized that she wasn't just Glynis Reed, but she was the Glynis Reed engaged to the president's son.

"Both of our families are forever in her debt for saving my life."

"That's my Cree," West announced as he approached from behind. He wrapped his arms around my waist and kissed my neck. "I see you didn't waste any time at all making friends, luv."

"You two are an item?" Clarissa gawked. She was so getting some free desserts too.

"She may very well one day be Lady Archer if all goes as planned," West announced, and I pinched his arm resting around my waist beneath the bar top. See, I could be discreet. If lightning was going to strike him down, I didn't want to be scalded for one of his lies. If I was going down, it would be by my own devious deeds.

I sounded special. As special as both Glynis and West were in the head. Each had spun an impossibly unbelievable tale. The lies were getting as thick as the layers I used to frost my cakes. I couldn't decide whose made-up version of me was more ludicrous; fake dating a real lord or saving the president's son's fiancée and getting acknowledged for it.

"So does that mean you're going to have a nickname like Sparrow that the secret service uses?" I asked Glynis out of curiosity.

"Songbird." She grinned. "You truly had no idea whose life you saved. That's even more fascinating."

"You and Lord Archer simply must sit at our table during the fundraiser." Priscilla lifted her glasses again to prop them on her head.

"Sorry, but she's already sitting at ours. I'm hoping if I get her tipsy enough, she'll agree to make my wedding cake," Glynis said.

Patricia pushed her empty glass away and slid off the stool. Clarissa was quick to follow. "It was a pleasure, Cree. I look forward to chatting tonight over drinks."

Wasn't that what we'd just done?

"Sure." I smiled as Priscilla wove her arm around Clarissa's arm and walked away with their heads together like they were plotting how to stab me through the heart so Clarissa could sink those long claws into Lord Archer.

"Okay, you two. Don't you think that was a little thick? You made me sound like a cross between Mother Teresa and the Queen of England."

"I saw the way their attitude switched to ice cubes, and I thought I could help thaw their veins. You remember the saying, 'you always want what you can't have'? I just helped make you irresistible and someone they couldn't have."

"Now they want you in their circle, even if just out of spite," West added.

"Dad told me why you were here, and technically, my story was true," Glynis said, taking another sip of her drink. "You are getting a pretty pin for saving my life, and I hope you'll come to my wedding, even if you don't agree to bake the cake."

"And she is marrying the president's son," West added.

"And you?" I spun to face him as he took a stool on the other side of me. "What's your excuse?"

"I figured if we said we were together, there would be fewer men hitting on you and you'd be able to focus on the answers we're after."

I gasped. Seriously?

"You are rocking the bikini," Glynis added. "Three men have already walked by trying to get your attention, and you didn't even look twice. You aren't good in the flirting department, are you?"

"I'm not here to flirt." My voice sounded whiny to my own ears, so I took another sip of the expensive wine. It went down my throat like melted ice cream on a hot Sunday afternoon. "I can't believe my cover is blown. They know who I am. They'll figure out why I'm here now, and no one is going to talk to me."

"They would have figured it out eventually during the cocktail party when we mingled." West rubbed my back. "Does that mean we can leave?"

I gawked at him. "No."

"Then chin up," Glynis said, sliding off her stool. "I always wanted to play detective. I'll help you; just tell me what you need."

I shrugged as my wheels started to spin. What I needed to figure out was who'd written that note and who the hell Davina really was. "I need writing samples from the people in Davina's life, and I need to figure out her true identity. She had several IDs."

"Leave the writing samples to me. I can be very persuasive when I want to be."

"You'd do that?" I asked. Hope seeped from my voice.

"Of course." She smiled. "I'll see you two at the cocktail party."

West and I both watched Glynis leave. She wiggled her fingers as a couple walked past her. She had a style and grace that I hadn't witnessed while using *Insight*. She wasn't stuck up or a snob, two things I expected in abundance from this trip.

"You two became fast friends."

"I saved her life. It's possible she thinks she owes me." I shrugged. "Nice girl, though. I'm glad I didn't chicken out sending that anonymous letter to her dad."

"Who do we need to talk to next?"

"Logan, the fiancé, his friends, the senator, anyone associated with Davina, which I'm guessing isn't many people. I should really call Freddie and Faraday to have them double-check Priscilla and Clarissa's alibis. Those two women didn't seem very fond of Davina."

"I'll do it," West said, pulling out his phone. He nodded his head toward Mason Spencer headed our way. "You have incoming at one o'clock. I'll give you some privacy and meet you back in our room."

"Thanks."

Chapter 10

Leonard Mason Spencer ordered bottled water from the bartender and took a seat next to me. I waited until the bartender left my bill to walked away before I spoke.

"Leonard."

"Only my grandma calls me that, Cree," Mason said, twisting the top off the water. "How are you, Blue?"

"You'd know if you returned any of my calls."

The silence between us was deafening as the minutes ticked by without either of us speaking. His jaw tensed as he picked at the label on the bottle. I was making him uncomfortable. I must have forgotten to pack my I-give-a-shit bathing suit. Suffer.

"I'm an ass, I'll admit it. I meant to call." He cleared his throat and finally glanced my way.

He'd meant to call. How utterly crappy and he was lying on top of that. No goosebumps rose on my arms, no tingles in my gut. Jerk. Oh, I wasn't letting him off the hook that easy. I deserved an answer.

"Why didn't you?" I twisted the fabric of the sarong between my fingers. Did I even want to hear his answer?

He sighed. "What I need to say and what I want to say are two very different things."

"Oh, for crying out loud." I slid off the stool. "Man up, already, Mason. It's simple. Cree, I'm not interested. Cree, you're a freak. Cree, my job is more important right now." I gulped the rest of my wine because that was some expensive stuff, and I wasn't leaving any behind. "Any of those things would have been better than intentional silence."

He turned his whole body to face me. "It's not that simple. I like you. I wanted to try, but other things in my life need my attention."

Goosebumps. He was telling the truth. I lifted the veil for answers, tired of the confusing excuses and games Mason was playing. I asked my guide what it was that was so important. His daughter flashed in my mind. "Your daughter?"

"My ex threatened to sue for full custody if I date you or bring you anywhere around our daughter. She doesn't understand that you aren't a charlatan, that you're the real deal. I know that, but she read the papers. She blames you for Moreno getting out of jail. The whole town does. I just can't…" He lowered his head.

"You just can't take that chance," I answered for him. The only thing I needed him to do was believe in me and in our potential. I couldn't hate him for caring about his daughter more than me. I couldn't even be angry he'd chosen family over me. My heart tightened, and I swallowed around the lump in my throat. I just had to go and push the issue. Still, knowing the problem was better than being left in the dark.

Would I ever be right for anyone? Would I ever be truly accepted? I let out a deep breath and rested my hand on his shoulder. "I get it, Mason. It's okay." Those words tasted like sludge on my tongue. "I would have done the same thing."

He lifted his head and met my gaze. "No, you wouldn't have. You would have found a way. You would have made it work. That's who you are. I just can't. I was already falling for you. If I stayed, if I put in the effort and tried, I'd fall the rest of the way, and I couldn't handle having to choose. You'd both own a piece of my heart, and it would never be whole again."

I rested my hand on his cheek. "You're a good dad, and a great man, Mason Spencer. Don't let anyone ever tell you different."

"So that's it? I just walk away?"

"Well, we've tried dating and working together." I chuckled at the thought. "Maybe we should try friends."

Mason turned his head into my hand and kissed my palm. "I'd like that." He pushed to his feet to tower over me and pulled a folded piece of paper out of his pocket. "Her real name was Dina Short."

I opened the paper to find a printed copy of all the IDs I'd found with the Dina ID circled. "How?"

"Reed told me what you were working on and I called my old chief and ran her face through facial recognition before we came. Dina Short used to work at the same bank where the museum was storing some rare coins in a safety deposit box. Those coins went missing and she was a suspect. They couldn't ever pin it on her. The security cameras were disabled, and there was no proof. She even had a solid alibi. They think it was a two-person job, someone on the inside with access to steal the coins and a hacker who took the system down, giving her the opportunity to steal the contents of the box. The coins have never been recovered."

I glanced down at the paper. "She must have sold some of them. That would explain the cash in the backpack."

"It gets better. The senator sits on the board for the bank where Davina worked and where the coins were stolen."

My gaze shot up to his. "Do you think he was in on it?"

He shook his head. "I doubt it. The museum was having work done on their security system, so the curator obtained that box and several others to hold some of their valuables while the workers were in and out of the building. It's ironic. They'd picked the bank for better security for the precious coins."

"If there isn't another tie besides just the senator sitting on the board, then it doesn't make sense. What's the connection I'm missing?"

"I'm not sure." He held my gaze. "But whatever you find, promise me you'll use that pretty brain of yours and not get hurt."

"Thanks." I refolded the paper. "This will help."

"What are friends for?" The smile didn't reach his eyes. "They're sending me on another assignment, so I'm on my way out. I just didn't want to leave before we had a chance to talk."

"If you have another assignment, then why were you here to begin with?"

"Deputy Director Reed thought I might be able to keep you out of trouble because of our history."

Our history. I gave him a sad smile and rested my hand over his heart, feeling the strength of each beat. Mason was a good man. He was husband potential, just not mine. I tapped his chest with my fingers. "This is where it matters, Mason. She's your heart. I was just a passing visitor."

Mason rested his hand on top of mine as he leaned down to kiss my cheek. "You were far more than that, Blue. Keep in touch."

"I should be saying that to you."

"I'll do better. I promise."

Mason turned, and with one last smile over his shoulder, he waved before disappearing back inside the hotel.

****

I'd come looking for answers. I might not have been planning to run into Mason, but at least now I knew exactly where he stood. I ran my hands down the black cocktail dress and checked once more for lipstick on my teeth. I wanted to be here, right? I'd chosen to investigate. Why the hell did I even think I'd fit in with this bunch of people, much less figure out who killed Davina?

I threw open the bedroom door to find West lounging on the bed, dressed in his suit, minus the jacket and shoes with a computer on his lap. "The fed came through for you. These priceless coins put a whole new spin on things."

"Why am I doing this? I'm not a private investigator. I'm not a cop. I'm not trained to deal with this crap."

West finally lifted his gaze from the computer to look at me. "You do this because helping people is who you are. Why are you having a change of heart?"

I plopped down on the bed and laced my fingers together. "I'm not normal. I mean I live with an almost retired cop and an ex-mobster. Who does that? Nothing in my life is normal."

West slid off the bed. "Normal is overrated. But you know what is normal? Baking desserts. That's about as American as your reality shows."

I met his gaze. "Maybe I should have stayed in the shadows, sent my anonymous letters, and just created desserts."

He dropped to his knees in front of me and took my hands. "So make this your new normal. This is who you are. You're smart, and you're gifted in more ways than making food. You speak for the victims when they can't. I can't think of a nobler gift than that. So own it, Lady Blue. Be who you were meant to be and fly your crazy flag for all to see."

"You're just saying that because you don't want me to quit before I solve your case."

"I'm saying that because not everyone is brave enough to step out of the box and ignore their own fears of other people's opinions and follow their true path. Be you, no one else."

"Own it." I sighed. He was right.

"Be brave," he added and pushed to stand, holding out his hand.

I took it and let him pull me up. "That's easy to say coming from the super-secret spy lord."

"You're right. Of course, it should be easy for the super-psychic, mystery-solving, recipe-inventing southern belle who talks to the dead. Be you, Cree. I happen to like her."

A smile split my lips as I looked up at him. "I may embarrass you."

"God, I hope so." He leaned down, his lips hovered a breath away. "There's nowhere else I'd rather be."

Confusion clouded my erratically beating heart. "Don't kiss me."

His lips twisted at the corners. His eyes sparkled. "I can wait till you're over the fed."

He stepped back, giving me room to breathe.

"Maybe I should become a nun. Do they believe in the supernatural, or do you think I'd get shunned there too?"

"I'm not sure. If I ever meet one, I'll be sure and ask." West put on his shoes and slipped into his coat jacket. He looked dashing in a 007 kind of way. I bet he had a stick of chewing gum he could use to blow through doors or even a pair of x-ray glasses stashed inside. I wanted to play.

"Are you ready Lord Archer?"

"Absolutely, Lady Blue."

I laughed as I grabbed my purse and we both headed for the door. The walk to the hotel was cloaked in darkness. Even the moon hid behind the clouds. The path was dotted with circles of light from the few lampposts along the way. The salty breeze from the ocean calmed my nerves and surprisingly made me feel a bit more heightened not only with my crazy emotional roller coaster ride but just deep inside. I could feel the vibrations down to my core getting stronger and grabbing hold.

Visions of an older man lying sick on a bed popped into my head. An older woman was by his side, and a younger man was kneeling bedside. Behind him was a red-headed woman resting a comforting hand on his shoulder. Two men stood in the shadows of the castle. I barely saw the glint of the guns.

I slowed to a stop, speechless, as Calinda Sparks reappeared. *He must leave now, or he won't be able to stop it. The time is near.*

"When does this happen?"

"Cree, are you okay?"

Twenty-four hours near the west corridor.

I shook my head. "Is the prince married?"

"To Katherine. Why?"

"Does she have red hair?"

"Yes. What's going on?"

"You have to go. We have to get you packed." I kicked off my heels and grabbed them. Turning, I jogged back to the cabana. I threw open the door and grabbed his suitcase and tossed it on the bed. I was pulling his clothes out of the closet when he walked in.

"What are you doing?"

"Phillip and his dad, the king. If you leave now, you'll make it in time."

His eyes widened, and his mouth parted as I hurried into the bathroom and grabbed his toiletries. I sat them on the bed. He stood immobile, still, as if trying to process my words. He didn't have time to wait. I grabbed his phone and scrolled to the last number that wasn't local, only momentarily pausing on Freddie's digits. I scrolled past it and dialed the long distance number as I zipped up the bag.

"West, thank God," a female answered, her voice barely a whisper.

"Sorry, not West. This is Cree. You must be Katherine."

"Where's West? It's urgent I speak with him."

"There's about to be an attempt on your lives. Hang on and let me give him the phone so I can finish getting him packed. Tell him what you know, and he'll be there soon."

I handed the phone to West, who looked at it like he hadn't a clue what to do with it. I rested my hand on his cheek, and he stared into my eyes. "They need you. Now focus."

He nodded and put the phone to his ear. "Katherine."

West walked to the window while I hurried around the room, grabbing his things and shoving them into his other bag. By the time he got off the phone, I had him packed and his stuff waiting by the door. I'd drawn a crude map of everything I'd seen bits of pieces around where the men were lying in wait to kill the royal family, but not enough to pinpoint.

"I..."

"You have to go. It's okay."

"How will you get back?"

"Don't worry about me." I slid his bag over his shoulder and pulled the suitcase handle out and shoved it in his hand. "Just go."

"How did you know?"

"Stop asking stupid questions. You're wasting time. Now go." I shoved my drawing into his hands.

I slipped into my shoes and practically pulled him out the door. "Be careful. I only saw two, but there could be more. I think they're planning to overthrow Phillip and his family."

"I can't leave you."

"You can, and you will. Now go, or so help me, I won't help you solve Calinda's murder."

Determination filled his eyes seconds before he leaned down and pressed his lips to mine. As nice as the kiss was, his warm lips were gone in a flash. "Don't do anything stupid."

"No promises."

Chapter 11

I took a deep breath stepping inside the cocktail party being held in one of the banquet rooms. The lights were dim. Soft music filled the air as men and women mingled around the room with drinks in their hands. Men with ear pieces guarded the door and were strategically placed. I didn't fit in with this crowd. I only knew a handful of people in attendance.

Senator Channing and his wife stood near the orchestra stage talking to a group of people. I headed for the nearest bar, bypassing the waiter carrying what looked to be champagne. To make it through tonight, I needed a clear head. I smiled at the bartender. "Can I get a club soda?"

He filled my order before I found a quiet place to watch my surroundings. A quick glance at my watch confirmed that I had only a few hours before the party would die down.

Glynis caught my eye and smiled, sliding away from the party conversation. "You made it. I was beginning to wonder." She glanced around. "Where's your date?"

"He had an emergency and had to leave."

"Even better," she said, stopping a passing waiter. She took the drink from my hands and laid it on the tray and grabbed two champagne flutes. "I have some people you'll want to meet."

"I'm not here to enjoy myself."

She leaned in to whisper as she steered me across the room. "You need to get inside the circle to ask questions, right? How about we start with some of Logan's closest friends? I've already been supplying them with shots to loosen their lips."

"I like the way you think." I grinned and sipped my champagne as she led me out of the room and into an adjoining room where a younger crowd had gathered. A pool table sat across the room. A couple of men had shrugged out of their jackets and were playing a game while even more looked on. Their laughter carried around the room.

A guy I recognized sat alone at one table. He wasn't a personal acquaintance, but his face was unmistakable. It had been on the cover of *Sizzle Magazine*. He'd been named one of the internet's hottest computer geeks who had recently sold his company for a billion dollars.

"He's one of Logan and Clarissa's friends. I can introduce you," Glynis teased. "But he's not one of the guys you need to talk to."

"Okay." I scanned the group she was leading me toward. "Fellas, I'd like to introduce you guys to Cree. She's new to the island, and her date was unexpectedly called away."

I watched as their eyes slid down my body. One might have even licked his lips.

"His loss is our good fortune." The brunette lifted his beer mug, and some sloshed over the side.

"Ignore him. He'll be passed out within the hour. I, on the other hand, would be honored to be your date," a man with a beautifully familiar face and blond hair announced.

"Cree, this is Charlie."

"Have I seen you somewhere before?"

"Have you been to the movies lately?" Glynis asked.

"Not really."

Charlie held his hand to his chest like I'd shoved a knife straight through his heart. "We'll have to rectify that."

"He's had three box office hits," Glynis said, sipping her champagne.

"He's not the man for you." Dark-hair-with-dangerously-sexy-eyes announced, sliding behind the bar. "He'll bore you with his acting, but I could make you forget all about your loser date by singing you a song that will mend your heart and melt your panties."

"Cree, this is Butler Spade, lead singer of Force Fire."

I was in testosterone overload. "Sorry, I've never heard of you either."

Butler's mouth parted, and he turned his gaze to Glynis. "Where did you find her?"

"That's my secret." Glynis grinned.

Three hours later they'd had several more shots, and our little side party had moved into one of the penthouse suites, complete with stocked kitchen and servants. They were raiding the fridge when I started pulling out ingredients for my favorite cookies and started to whip the recipe together. I'd just shoved them into the oven, and all the guys were taking turns dipping their fingers into the bowl.

Glynis walked behind the guys and point-nodded toward Charlie, the blond actor. "So, Charlie, I heard you were supposed to be Logan's best man."

Charlie could hardly focus his eyes. "I knew it wouldn't last."

"Why's that?" I asked, cleaning out the bowl.

"She was stepping out on him," Butler announced.

"If she was still playing the field, then why were they getting married?"

"Because she played the ultimate ball-and-chain card, the one that screws him for eighteen years," Charlie answered, propping his head in his hand.

Glynis and I shared a look. "She was pregnant?"

"She even tried to hide it from him at first, but he found the pregnancy stick."

Oh, Davina. She was a naughty girl. Secret identity, stolen coins, and a hidden pregnancy. Not that I was one to judge. She sounded like her life was a billion times more interesting than mine.

"I bet the baby wasn't even his, but enough about her," Butler said, meeting my gaze. "Tell us about you."

"Oh, there's not much to tell. I was just someone's plus one."

"Nonsense," Glynis interjected. "She's psychic, and she single-handily saved my life."

"Actually I wasn't even there."

"Well, you told my dad who the killer was. I'm giving you all the credit."

"You're psychic?" I read the skepticism on Butler's face. "Prove it."

I didn't normally perform on command. Spirits had a way of just giving me enough information to be dangerous, but I'd been ignoring the spirits in the room since we walked in. The timer went off, and I pulled the cookies from the oven and turned it off.

One of the spirits hovered near Butler, holding an old acoustic guitar and wearing a Force Fire T-shirt. "You lost a band member."

"You could have read that in the paper."

"Fair enough," I said and looked at the spirit again. "Did your band member play acoustic guitars? Because that's what he's holding."

"Lucky guess. Reggie played the electric guitar on stage."

Reggie. I glanced at the player and spoke out loud. "You're going to have to give me something a bit more helpful."

Reggie grinned. *Tell him the new song, Butcher Block, is in the wrong key and to change it to D major for a better flow. Once he does, he'll have a new hit single. He also needs to take back the blue baby outfit he bought for his sister and exchange it for pink.*

A long time ago I tried to quit making sense out of messages I'd received. I'd be locked away in a looney bin if I let my OCD take over trying to understand all the impertinent nonsense. I relayed the message and watched the suspicion in his eyes grow into intrigue."

"No one knows about that song or that my sister is pregnant. No one."

I shrugged. "He does."

"This is fabulous," Charlie said, grabbing several of my cookies and passing them out to the others. He took a bite. "Do me."

"This is the last one." I glanced around the room when a spirit stepped forward holding up two screenplays. One was entitled *Death Charge* and the other *Just Once*. He tossed *Death Charge* to the ground and stomped on it before enthusiastically pointing to the other. Visions of a red carpet and screaming fans filled my mind.

"I don't know who this guy is, but he's showing me two screenplays. He's indicating he doesn't want you to do *Death Charge* but seems to be really excited about one called *Just Once*."

"Holy shit," he exclaimed, sitting up straighter like what I'd just told him had knocked the liquor-induced stupor from his body. "I was just issued a contract on *Death Charge* to sign tomorrow."

I tisked. "I'd probably reconsider if I were you. Spirits won't lead you astray." Would they? I mean, technically, who really knew if these guys were out for our greater good or to have one last laugh as we stumbled?

"If you're right, I'm going to make you my new manager and my new best friend."

"Stand in line. I found her first," Glynis announced, finishing off her cookie.

"Technically, I found you." I chuckled and turned my attention back to the guys. "So if Davina was having an affair, who do you guys think she was messing with?"

They exchanged a look and grinned before Butler answered. "Senator Channing."

Chapter 12

The sound of my phone vibrating on the table pulled me from my sleep. I flicked on the light and glanced at the clock. Eight a.m.

The number calling read blocked. "Yeah?"

"Cree, this is Mason."

I plopped back down on my pillow and wiped the sleep from my eyes. "When I said keep in touch, I should have mentioned that I like to sleep in. You're like one of those obnoxiously happy morning people, aren't you?"

He chuckled. "And you're quite the night owl. I heard you made quite the impression last night."

"And here I thought everyone I talked too was too drunk to remember."

"Actually, you made the news again just this morning, only this time it was the entertainment news."

"What?" I shot up in the bed, making my head spin. "How? Who?"

"Actor Charlie Gallows' manager announced that Charlie turned down a multimillion-dollar deal for a leading role, and he credited you for helping to influence that decision."

"Crap."

"His fans are going to be pissed."

I plopped back down on my pillow. "They can join the crowd."

"That's not why I'm calling though. Yesterday, you mentioned Davina had a bunch of money from possibly pawning a coin. As I boarded a boat to leave the island, I ran with your suggestion and called Faraday and asked him to check into the two pawn shops in town."

I rested my arm over my eyes to block a forming headache. "He found something, didn't he?"

"Yeah. He lucked out at the first one he hit. He pulled the surveillance, and it wasn't just

Davina that pawned the coin. She had some guy with her."

"Any chance they caught his face?"

"Faraday said the guy was wearing a green hoodie with some type of boating emblem on it and a hat to hide his face. He kept his head down the entire time."

"Of course he did." I let out a disgruntled sigh. "Approximate age? Height? Anything?"

"Faraday is technology challenged, so I have a call into the PD's forensic team to send me a copy after he drops it off. I'll forward it to you as soon as I get it."

"Thanks, Mason. I appreciate your help."

"Watch your back, Cree. Those coins are worth a billion dollars, and if those coins are the motive, then someone has a billion reasons to keep you quiet."

"I've got enough motives to write a movie. Between the coins, the affair, and a hidden pregnancy, there were plenty of reasons to want Davina silenced. The questions are, which reason was she killed over and who pulled the trigger? The jealous wife, the angry fiancé, the baby daddy, or maybe even someone she double-crossed over the coins. I don't even know where to start."

"Go back to the beginning and start with the evidence. Eliminate each until you find the one that you can't."

"I will. Thanks again for your help." I hung up and silently tried to remember everything about the *Insight* viewing.

Davina had been at the church and lied to the fiancé before heading to meet someone in a cabin when she got a call on a burner phone. She'd been ready to jump off the bridge but decided against it before being shot in the back and tumbling to her death. I found her IDs and the money later. That was all I originally started with.

I could speculate all day, but time was ticking to kick up some dust. I shrugged the covers off and got out of the bed. If I was going to confront people today, I needed copious amounts of coffee to be more alert. A morning swim and coffee would do the trick.

I changed into my bathing suit, grabbed a towel, my wallet, and the cabana key as I headed out. A groan rumbled in my chest as I checked my watch; only eight thirty in the morning. Gah.

I headed up the path, passing the other cabanas on the way. A door opened and startled me. The senator stepped out, walking backward, wearing jogging shorts and running shoes, and he was in a lip lock with no one other than Clarissa. I glanced around me, looking for a place to duck when there was nowhere to go. I stood motionless as they broke the kiss and Clarissa eased the door shut. The senator turned and spotted me. He cleared his throat and zipped up his light jacket. A real runner wouldn't have been wearing a jacket like that in the 100-degree weather where humidity was close to hitting the temperature in hell. "I didn't see you there."

"Obviously," I said and started to walk past him, only he kept in step with me.

"It's not what it looks like."

"Yeah, I'm sure Clarissa was helping you get quite a workout." I held up my hand. "I'm not here to judge."

"You're Cree Blue, right?"

"Yep. This is a lovely island. Thanks for the invite."

He grabbed my arm to stop me. "How much is it going to take to make you forget you saw that and not run to the press?"

I yanked my arm from his grasp and crossed my arms over my chest. "I don't want your money. I want answers."

"Okay. She and I started…"

I held up my hand. "I don't care about you and her. It's obvious you have an affinity for younger women. The only answer I want is if you were having an affair with your son's fiancée."

"Davina? Why would you ask that?"

"I'm sure the authorities will find out soon enough when they do the autopsy and run

DNA on her unborn child. Were you aware she was pregnant?"

The senator ran his hand through his wet hair. "No, I wasn't."

"Where were you the day she was killed?"

His brows dipped. "You want my alibi?"

"Either that or I can get it from Priscilla when I talk to her about Clarissa. I'm sure that will go over real well."

"I can promise you that she won't care. She knows I have trysts; she has them too." He crossed his arms.

"So did one of your trysts include Davina?"

"I met Davina when I was touring one of the banks where I sit on the board, only then her name wasn't Davina. It was Dina."

"So you're aware she was using an alias?"

"Of course I was. I helped her establish it."

I was rendered speechless.

"She was going to ruin me. She had compromising pictures from our affair."

"So you were in on the coin heist?"

"What?"

"The missing museum coins from the bank."

"No." He ran his hand through his hair and lowered his gaze. "I mean she knew about the coins in the deposit box, but that was pillow talk. A lot of people knew about those coins. We discussed them at dinner parties. We even had them on display at one of our museum fundraisers." He met my gaze. "Are you suggesting she's the person that took them?"

"Where in all this crazy drama did Logan meet Davina?"

"I introduced them. She was a guest on the island."

I glanced at Clarissa's cabana. It was convenient he used this place to have his little love fests. It was away from prying eyes.

"I guess she chose the younger option."

"Your guess is as good as mine. She broke things off with me, and she and Logan started dating after the fundraiser. Two months later he'd proposed to her."

"Why wouldn't you warn your son about who she is?"

"Davina was bright and beautiful and she had a way about her that brings out the good in those around her. I think that was why I found her so alluring. I'd thought about warning Logan about who she really was, but then I would have had to tell him how exactly I knew. I watched his back and made sure his bases were covered. I'm the one that insisted he get a prenup."

"Did Logan know about your affair?"

"God no." The senator took me by the elbow and started leading me toward the pools. "No one knew about that affair, and I'd like to keep it that way. It would destroy Logan if he ever found out."

"I'm going to ask you one more time, Senator. Where were you the day Davina was killed?"

"I was in Washington at a conference. My constituents can vouch for me."

I needed coffee. Didn't these people understand that my mind wasn't fully operational at this time in the morning? I cracked my neck from side to side and stopped him with a palm on his arm. "Look me in the eye and tell me you didn't kill her."

"I didn't kill my Davina, Dina, or anyone."

Goosebumps. Damn it. He was telling the truth, and I was almost ready to pin the whole thing on him. "I believe you."

"So you'll keep my indiscretions to yourself?"

"I deal with dead people, Senator. Most of the ones that I meet and come into contact with are still lingering around because they have regrets and just want to find peace. So if you're unhappy, you should deal with it. Life is way too short not to find your version of peace while you're still alive to enjoy it. Now, this is a five-cups-of-coffee conversation and seeing how my cabana lacked a coffee pot, I'll leave it at that. Have a good day, Senator."

"You surprise me, Ms. Blue. I heard about what you did for Harrison Reed, so when he asked for your invite as a personal favor to him, I was a little reluctant."

"Why, because I'm psychic?"

He chuckled. "No, because you were in the papers for handing a mob boss a get-out-of-jail-free card. Associations with people like that, not matter how distant, tend to be remembered."

"Gah. Isn't a slashed tire and hate mail enough already?" I shook my head and headed for the bar. God, I hope they had a coffee pot hidden somewhere that worked. "When are people going to let that go?"

"In my line of business, that's easy to answer. When a bigger story than you finds the headlines and they find someone else to target their emotions on."

He snapped his fingers, and a bartender appeared in front of us. "Get Ms. Blue a coffee and anything else she wants free of charge during the rest of her stay."

"That's not necessary, Senator." I leaned into him as the bartender worked on my coffee at the end of the bar. "I told you that you don't have to buy me off."

"I remember," he whispered back. "I'm doing this because I want to."

"I might bankrupt you with just the coffee orders." I chuckled as the bartender returned with an extra-large coffee, not a tiny one in a little teacup.

"Enjoy your stay, Ms. Blue."

I picked up my coffee and put it straight to my lips, sipping it. I waved my hand as I walked away.

That was easy enough. Why hadn't I thought of that earlier? I'd just find a central location, and what better place to wait than by the pool? Eventually, most of my suspects might come walking by. I'd just ask each person and eliminate each one judging by my goosebumps. Too bad I couldn't ask them about the stolen coins since everyone who attended that fundraiser had seen them. I'm not sure I could trust my goose bumps unless I worded the question just right.

I sat my coffee cup down and spread out my towel before plopping my butt down on the chair. The warmth of the sun already promised another sweltering day.

I went through three cups of coffee and was on my second dip in the pool to cool off before I spotted the first signs of life; too bad it wasn't one of my suspects.

Deputy Director Harrison Reed sat down on the chair next to mine and unfolded his newspaper. "You've been a busy girl."

I rested my arms on the side of the pool and let my body float in the water. "I promise I have no idea what you're talking about."

He flipped his paper around to show me the headline. A picture of Charlie was on the front page. "Oh that. When did he possibly have time to call his manager?"

"Your secret has gone nationwide now that Charlie has nicknamed you America's Sweetheart and his personal psychic. I'm starting to believe that you're going to need your own protection detail."

"Nah," I said and pushed off the wall to float on my back. "The world just needs another scandal to forget all about me. The senator already explained how it works."

"So what's on your agenda today?"

I swam over to the steps and climbed out of the pool. "I plan to ask everyone if they killed Davina."

His mouth parted, and he stared at me. "Are you expecting one of them to confess?"

DEADLY VOWS

Chapter 13

"I'll be able to tell if they're lying."

"Have you been watching Discovery ID and been taking notes on how to interrogate?"

"Not quite. I get goosebumps when I'm being told the truth. No goosebumps equals a lie."

"And you've tested this theory?"

"Sure. You want me to test you?"

"Nope, and I'm afraid all of your suspects are scheduled off the island for a while."

"You're fibbing."

"Did your goose bumps tell you that?"

"I wasn't paying attention. Tell me again."

He repeated what he said, and goose bumps physically appeared on my arms. I may have cursed like a mother trucker. Okay, more like a person who stubbed her toe on the bed in the dark. But what the heck. I'd been up since eight and looking forward to uncovering the truth. How was I going to do it now with all of my suspects gone?

"Where did they go?"

"To the Billson Police Department for questioning and to schedule funeral arrangements for Davina. They promised to be back for the fundraiser and to start making transportation arrangements back to the mainland for everyone first thing in the morning."

My mouth fell open. "Get out. Do they know who the killer is?"

"I think they're getting close to an arrest."

"Huh." I sat down in my chair. "How is it you're friends with these people? I mean don't get me wrong, I'm sure they're fabulous in their own sweet convoluted ways with their lies, deceit, and the way they throw money around like I do spices. But what gives?"

"Priscilla and I go back to college days. She was the athletic type and played several sports. She was on the female row team, and I was on the men's. We shared mutual friends."

The boat insignia. Hadn't Mason said that the person in the video had a boat insignia when they pawned the coin? "Do you have any pictures of your glorious college rowing days?"

"I don't, but Priscilla has one hanging up in the office. Would you like to see?"

I sprang from my chair and wrapped my towel around my body. Obviously, my coffee picked that moment to kick in. "Absolutely. Should I go change first?"

"No, that's okay. We don't have to go to the lobby. She has a pool entrance that we can use."

I grabbed my stuff and refastened my watch as I walked in step with Harry leading me to the door. He twisted the knob, and to my surprise, it opened right up. "They must feel pretty safe to leave offices unlocked."

"Well, we are on their personal island and have agents around every corner."

"True." I stepped inside and was met by a gush of cool air, so I pulled my towel tighter around my body.

He walked over to one of the walls and pointed to the picture that depicted a combination of men and women on a rowing team. Each had on a green blazer, each with a boat emblem. "You both graduated from the same school?"

"Not only Priscilla and I, but it's a family tradition. All of our kids have graduated from our alma mater. Logan and Glynis attended, although they graduated different years."

I walked down the sea of green blazers and looked closer at the photos until I picked out Logan. Even though I hadn't met him yet, he looked just like I remembered from using Insight. "Logan hasn't changed much. Did you guys happen to get green hoodies with the matching emblems?"

"Yeah, they were part of our training uniforms. What are you getting at, Cree?"

"Mason." I paused, remembering who I was talking to. "Sorry, Agent Spencer called me this morning. That's why I was up so early; anyway, he said that there was a video of Davina fencing a stolen coin that I believe she stole from the bank where she worked. Long story short, there was someone in the video with her." I pointed to the picture of ugly green blazers. "Wearing a hoodie that matches this emblem that you, Priscilla, and Logan all had during your training days. Only there was no clear shot of her accomplice's face."

"You say Mason has video?"

"He's supposed to send it to me so I can take a look, but I haven't gotten it yet."

"Excuse me a second, and I'll make a call to get that expedited." He stepped out of the office toward the pool, leaving me alone.

The phone buzzed in my hand, and I glanced at the caller ID, hoping that it was

Mason sending me the video, but the caller ID read West.

I chuckled. When had he entered his number into my phone? "Do you make it a habit of inserting your number into other people's phones? How did you get around my security code?"

"It's your birthday. You should probably change that," he said.

"How are the royals? Did you make it in time to ruin the mutiny?"

"I did. They send their regards and very much would like to meet you. They've requested that I invite you to visit the castle as their guest of honor, complete with a formal ball and everything."

"No thanks. I've had my fill of celebrities to last me a lifetime." I slowly walked down the walls of pictures that depicted Priscilla's college years. I paused at the picture of her and nine other women holding professional looking sniper rifles with a trophy sitting in front of the bunch. Priscilla was wearing a gold medallion for first place around her neck. "Holy crap. I know who killed Davina."

"Who?" West asked just as the phone was ripped out of my hand.

"Make a sound, and I'll blow your head off," Priscilla whispered in my ear. She hit the end button and tossed my phone on the ground, stepping on it with her shoe. "We're going to take a walk."

"I thought you had left." I whispered.

"Unlucky for you, they only wanted to talk to Preston and Logan."

"Why did you kill her?"

"She slept with my husband and wormed her way into my son's life. I wasn't going to let that tramp ruin everything I've built. Do you have any idea how hard it was to get to where I am today?"

"You're crazy if you think people won't miss me. Just let me go, and I won't tell anyone it was you." It was times like this that I really wished I'd been paying attention when Freddie was teaching me how to fight instead of just copying his moves to make him happy. "Harrison will be back any second and probably even faster if he hears gunfire."

She shoved the gun harder against my temple and yanked me to another door. She pulled it open and shoved me to the ground inside. "I can deal with Harrison. I'll tell him you left. He'll trust me. I'll be back tonight after the benefit to deal with you. Don't worry dear. I'll give you a send-off into a watery grave too."

She slammed the door, and I heard the unmistakable sound of a deadbolt.

This wasn't happening. Only Harrison knew I'd been in the office, and with my luck, he was going to believe Priscilla. Damn it. I shoved to my feet and started banging on the door.

I screamed until my voice was starting to go hoarse and my fist started to ache. I glanced at my watch. The ball was scheduled to begin in three hours. I had to find a way to get out.

DEADLY VOWS

West

Chapter 14

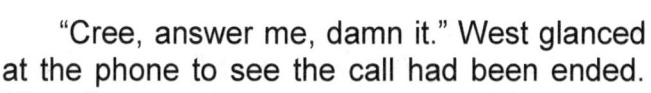

"Cree, answer me, damn it." West glanced at the phone to see the call had been ended. "Crap."

"What's wrong?" Phillip asked as he entered the room.

"Cree figured out the killer when I was talking to her, and then we got disconnected," West answered while trying to call her back. The call went straight to her voice mail.

"I'm sure she's fine."

He met Phillip's gaze. Anger stirred in his veins. "This is Cree Blue we're talking about.

The woman who is going to help us find the diamond. The same woman who managed to almost get herself killed."

"You're right. Try her again, and if that doesn't work, call the embassy or Harrison Reed. You need to find her."

West dialed Harrison's phone and received his voice mail too. "Goddamn it."

He started to pace, the way he did when worry consumed his thoughts. There was a big ocean separating them. Helplessly he scrolled through the numbers trying to find someone he trusted to help. "Freddie."

He dialed Freddie's number, and he answered on the first ring. "Tell me she's wearing her watch and you're watching her location."

"That's why I'm here. She was at the pool for several hours, and now she's in the hotel. What's wrong?"

"She figured out Davina's killer while I was on the phone with her, and the line cut off. She's in trouble. I can feel it."

"Calm down. I'll go check it out. It's pinging inside the hotel near the pool."

"You can't go. They'll kick you out since you weren't invited. They aren't even aware you're on the property. Just keep your eyes glued to the monitor, and I'll call you back."

"The fuck you say. I'm going in to get her."

"I just told you that security will throw you out. That place is swarming with feds. Sit tight, and I'll have Harrison call you and you can walk him directly to the location of her ping. Do not take your eyes off that monitor."

"Fine, five minutes is all you get. If you don't call me back, I'm going in, Archer."

Freddie hung up, and West tried Harrison's number again; voicemail. Crap.

"Tell me what you need," Phillip demanded, resting a calming hand on West's shoulder. "I'll make it happen."

"I need the president's soon-to-be daughter-in-law's phone number. Glynis Harrison."

Phillip picked up the phone, and there was a brief pause. "Get the President of the United States on the line. It's an emergency."

Within minutes, Phillip had the number and handed West. He dialed Glynis's number and walked to the window to look out over the ocean.

"Hello."

"Glynis, this is West Archer. We met."

"Right, the lord who ditched his date."

"I need you to listen to me very carefully. Cree is in trouble, and I need you to save her, but you can't walk into danger alone. Only take someone you trust. I have no idea if the killer has an accomplice."

"She figured out who it is?"

"Yes, and I can't reach your father. Do you have something to write with?"

"Uh…yeah." She grunted before speaking again. "Go ahead."

He gave her Freddie's number and explained that he would guide her to Cree's location.

"Got it."

"Be careful, Glynis."

She tisked. "I'll save her."

She hung up the phone, and he texted Freddie to expect Glynis's call and to direct her to where Cree was pinging from.

"I'm sure they'll find her," Phillip said.

"If they don't, and something happens to her…"

"She's smart and brave. They'll find her."

"They have to. Excuse me. I need to make arrangements to head back."

West walked out of the office and toward his room. He had to pack. He had to leave. If something happened to her, then that was on him. He should have never left her without someone sticking to her side. Damn it.

Chapter 15

I slowly scanned the items in the room. There wasn't much. An old wooden chair, a mop and a scratched-up desk. I rested my head back on my shoulders, and that was when I spotted my escape. An air vent on the ceiling.

I screeched the desk across the floor until it was right under the vent. I climbed up top, and it was still out of reach. I grabbed the mop and climbed back up, and using the mop handle, I pushed it open. I sighed in relief that it wasn't bolted down. "Yahtzee."

I hopped back down and grabbed the wooden chair and placed that on top of the desk. Slow and steady, I climbed back up and onto the chair. The legs beneath me wobbled as I grabbed the vent opening. My hands dug into the metal opening as the chair slipped beneath my feet and careened to the floor, breaking off one of the legs.

Sweat beaded my brow as my arms strained to hold my weight. "I swear on my father's grave, I will exercise more, train more, and learn to do a damn pull-up. Just let me get out of this."

I heard the deadbolt flick, and I tried to pull myself up into the vent, straining to lift my weight to no avail.

"Cree, are you in here?" Glynis whispered as the door opened.

"Oh thank God," I whispered.

She pushed the door farther open. Charlie and Butler were standing behind her.

"Now that's something you don't see every day," Charlie announced.

"Speak for yourself. Half-clad women try to climb up to my hotel balconies all the time," Butler said and moved farther into the room. He pushed the desk out of the way. "Drop."

I glanced down at his arms. "You'll drop me."

"We don't have much time. Drop, Cree."

"One, two...." I contained my squeal as I let go. Butler caught me without so much as a grunt. "Thanks."

"Come on. We need to get you out of here," Butler said and pulled his shirt over his head and handed it to me to use as a cover.

"How are we going to get out of here without her seeing us?"

"Who?" Glynis asked.

"Priscilla Channing," I whispered back.

"I just saw her in the ballroom ordering the staff around. Let's go out through the back," Butler said, pulling the cap off of Charlie's head. He slid it on top of mine and pulled me out of the room and out Priscilla's back door. "Charlie, you and Glynis go keep her occupied, and I'll sneak her down to my cabana."

"Got it," Glynis said and pulled Charlie out of the office.

Butler tossed his arm around me, and we slipped out the pool door. "Keep your head down and act casual. Anyone who's watching will think you're just another one of my flings."

I lowered my head as he rested his arm on my shoulders. We didn't slow, and we didn't falter as he steered me around the pool and toward the cabanas away from mine.

Without stopping, he handed me a drink. "She likes her liquor. Bill it to my room. Thanks, man."

I wanted to look up to see where he'd gotten it from but was afraid someone might recognize me.

"Where did you get this?" I whispered.

"From a passing waiter. I thought you might be thirsty."

"What is it?" I sniffed, and the smell of vodka smacked me in the nose.

He paused long enough to pull out his card key and use it in the lock before opening the door to usher me in. He closed the door behind us and quickly hurried around the room to close the blinds.

"That was close." He handed me his phone. "Call Freddie and tell him you're safe and sound."

"Freddie? How do you know who Freddie is?"

"Unless you want a massacre, you need to call him in the next…" He glanced at his watch. "Five minutes, or he's about to bust into the hotel with guns blazing."

I dialed Freddie's number and pressed the phone to my ear.

"Take your time. I'm going to go get you some clothes."

Freddie answered on the first ring. "Do you have her?"

"How did you know I was missing and where to find me?" I asked and walked to the window to peer out the blinds to make sure we weren't followed.

"Archer put a tracker in your watch. He said you were on the phone with him when you figured out the killer, but the call cut off."

I glanced at my watch. "I should have known super-secret spy guy had me bugged. What is it with the men in my life wanting to keep tabs on me?"

"Be glad he did, Cree, or you might be sleeping with the fishes."

I sighed and let the blinds drop back in place. "You should have told me you were here and about the watch."

"I know." His voice turned somber. "It kills me that he came up with the idea first. I wish I'd been the one to think of it."

"You and I are going to have a long talk about boundaries when I get back. Where are you by the way?"

"West chartered a boat for us, and we're on the other side of the island. He set us up in a little shack, but we're thankful it has running water and electricity."

"Who is 'us'?" I asked, resting my hand on my hip. So help me, if they'd pulled Charlotte into this, I was going to skin them alive or at least have my Grammy haunt their butts until they apologized.

"Jitters and the twins, Faraday is doing the leg work in town."

"All of you guys are in trouble." I turned to find Butler coming out of the bedroom with folded clothes in his hands. "Listen I've got to go change."

"What you need to do is come to me so I can get you the hell off this island. You figured out who the killer is. We'll tell the police and let them handle it."

"I need proof, or it's just my word against hers, and I haven't found the stolen coins yet."

"Cree, don't make me come get you."

I sighed. He was right, leaving the island and letting the cops handle it would be the smart thing to do. "I'll wait until dark and come to you. Where are you?"

"Up the beach about a mile from where you're currently located."

"Okay. I'll see you soon."

"Here you go." Butler handed me the clothes. "I'm not sure what will fit you, so I brought you an assortment. Wear whatever you want."

"Thanks." I pointed to his room. "Mind if I change in there?"

"Knock yourself out."

I headed for the room and plopped down on the bed. Realization of what had just happened punched me in the gut. The world was filled with lunatics disguised as normal everyday people. If everyday people consisted of hoity-toity, adulterous senators' wives that picked killing over common sense. It was kind of ironic that Priscilla would be the next scandal to replace my name in the papers.

Well, as long as they left my name out of the incident. I could only hope.

I changed into a Force Fire T-shirt that fell down to my knees. I slipped on a pair of his boxers beneath the shirt and folded them over at the waist to keep them from falling right off my body. I had curves, but damn.

I walked out of the bedroom to find Butler sitting in a chair with a guitar across his legs. He was strumming a song I'd never heard before. "That's beautiful."

"Too bad Force Fire doesn't have a reputation for slow lyrics."

I took a seat across the room. "Is that the song Reggie was telling you to change?"

"Yeah." Butler dropped his head and strummed the guitar and began to sing. His voice was like a fine wine on a Sunday afternoon. It soothed my soul and caressed my anxiety layers into comfortable ease.

"I love it. It's like comfort food for my soul." I announced.

Butler lifted his gaze, a smile stretched on his lips. "I do too, and that's a great name. I'll call it Soul Food. If that's okay with you."

"It's your song. You can call it whatever you want." I smiled.

A knock sounded on the door, and we both froze. Butler rose from his spot and peered out the blinds. He let out an audible sigh.

"It's just Glynis and Charlie."

He unlocked the door and let them in, closing and locking it behind them.

"I couldn't find my dad," Glynis announced. Worry etched her brow. "I can't even reach him by cell."

"I'm sure he's fine. Priscilla wouldn't hurt him."

"I called West and told him we had you. He would have saved you himself had he been nearby," Glynis said. "Personally, I think he's into you."

I waved my hand. "He wants help with a case."

Charlie sat down next to me and rested his arm on the back of the couch near my shoulders. "I never even met the guy, but I know he's into you. Take my word for it."

Heat claimed my cheeks until I remembered that Charlie was on my shit list. I glared at him. "You told the world I'm America's sweetheart and your personal psychic."

"Well, you are the only psychic I've met, and of course you're a sweetheart. You helped save Glynis and my career. I didn't lie."

My investigation into Davina's death had brought me to this specific moment in time. Here I was, sitting with the president's son's fiancée, a rock star, and a movie star. All that was missing was Charlotte. She would have loved every minute of this. My stomach picked that exact moment to grumble. Food hadn't been a priority earlier, but my stomach wasn't letting me forget. "Can I use your kitchen?"

"Are you making more cookies?" Charlie asked.

"I haven't eaten today."

"Relax. I'll fix you something." Butler rose from his seat and headed into the kitchen. I watched, trying to hide the worry from my face. What did the rock star know about cooking?

"Really, I can make myself something. You don't need to bother."

His laughter carried out into the living room. "I can promise it won't kill you. People say I'm a great cook."

"If by people you mean your nephew," Charlie called out.

"If it's not edible, I'll bring you back something from the dining area," Glynis whispered.

"Thanks." I gestured to her phone. "Do you have West's number?"

"Yeah, he called me when he couldn't reach my dad." She held it out. "Do you want to call him?"

I nodded and took her phone and headed to the bedroom. "I'll just be a minute."

I eased the door closed and scrolled through her calls until I found his number and hit the call button. He answered on the first ring.

"You got her, right?"

"If by her, you mean me, then yes, she found me."

"Cree." His concern turned to relief.

I stood in front of the dresser and toyed with Butler's watch while I spoke. "You put a tracker on me."

"I did, and I'm not sorry."

"You brought Freddie to the island."

"Guilty."

I put the watch back on the dresser. "Thank you."

There was a short pause. "What? No yelling? No arguing?"

I shook my head. "Not this time, but in the future, just so you know, all you had to do was ask. I know when I'm in over my head."

I sat down on the bed.

"I'm on my way back, but I've arranged an exit for you and Freddie. That was a smart choice to agree to leave."

"Even I can make a smart decision or two. It's not unheard of, you know."

He chuckled. "My flight arrives in five hours."

"That means you're on the plane now? How is that you're allowed to use your cell?"

"One of the many perks of having a prince as your best friend but don't worry. You'll get to experience it first-hand when we fly to California."

"Right." I'd almost forgotten that was why he'd found me so interesting. I glanced at the clock by the bed. The ball was still two hours away. I was about to look away when I spotted a coin. It was larger than a half-dollar and looked as though it were 100 years old. I picked it up and ran my finger over the scratched surface. "Listen. I'll just see you at my house when you land or tomorrow. I've got to go."

"Cree, I'll see you when I land."

"It's okay. I'll try to have everything wrapped up, and we can work on your stuff tomorrow or whenever, but I have to go."

"Fine, call me when you're home."

"I don't have a phone," I said and glanced at Butler's, which was sitting next to the coin. It was a burner phone just like the one Davina had been using.

"You will by the time I get there," he said.

"Sounds great. Really, though, I have to go."

"You sure you're okay?"

"Yeah," I answered and hung up when I heard the sound of the door opening behind me.

I spun around to find Butler standing in the doorway. "Your food is ready."

His gaze went to the coin in my hand, and he slowly started to walk toward me. "What are you doing with that?"

"I uh…"

He slipped it out of my hands and twisted it between his fingers. "It's my lucky coin. No one touches that."

"Right," I said, trying to slide around him.

His brows furrowed as he watched me. "Why are you acting like that?"

I grabbed the lamp from the dresser yanking the cord out of the wall. I held it like I might a bat, not that I played many sports. Okay, none. But I'd seen it on TV.

"Stay back." My voice came out as a shriek as I walked backwards toward the door, only stopping when Glynis and Charlie entered the room.

"What did you do to her?" Charlie asked.

He held up his coin. "She was holding my lucky coin. I just said no one was allowed to touch it, and she started acting like… that."

He pointed to me like I'd sprouted green skin and horns.

"Here, Cree, you can hold mine." Charlie pulled one out of his pocket and held it out.

I waved the lamp between the two of them. "You're in on it?"

"Cree, put the lamp down. I'm sure you're just rattled from earlier, and this is all just a misunderstanding."

Charlie held up his hands as he moved to the bed and put the coin on it. "You can take a look. There's nothing special about my coin."

I wasn't budging. "How did you two do it?"

"Do what?" Glynis asked.

"Steal the coins."

Charlie and Butler shared a look and laughed. Butler was the first to speak. "We didn't steal them; everyone in the wedding party got one."

I slowly shook my head. "From Davina?"

"No," Charlie answered. "From Logan."

I gestured to the phone. "And I suppose you want me to believe that disposable phone was a wedding present too?"

Butler picked it up and turned it on. He turned the screen for me to see. "My sister is pregnant, and she's had two miscarriages. It's her direct line to me. I sometimes ignore my personal phone since fans get the number. I won't ignore this phone. Only she has these digits."

"I don't believe you." I shook my head. I wasn't falling for this. I put my hand out to block Glynis and pushed her behind me, inching us closer to the door.

DEADLY VOWS

Chapter 16

"I'll prove it." Butler picked up the phone, hit a number, and put it on speaker.

A female answered. "Hey, Butler, why are you calling me from this number? It's only for emergencies. You haven't been arrested for something, have you?"

"I have you on speaker. Tell them your name."

"Tell who my name?" she asked.

"Just say your name," he growled.

"Winnie Spade-Mitchell." Her voice echoed through the silent room.

"And tell them why I have this phone."

"Butler, are you in trouble?"

"No, Winnie, just tell them why I have this particular phone, please."

"Because I'm pregnant." She growled in irritation. "Now you better tell me what the hell is going on before I bring my hormonal ass down there and kick some butts."

Charlie took the phone from Butler. "We're sorry, Winnie. This is Charlie. We thought Butler had a girlfriend he wasn't telling us about. That's all."

"Okay then. Butler, call me later when you're done screwing around with your friends. We need to discuss Mom and Dad's anniversary."

"I'll call you after I hit the mainland."

"Fine. Don't forget."

"I love you, Winnie Pooh," Butler said.

"I love you too, Butthead."

Butler disconnected the call and tossed the phone onto the bed. "Now your food is getting cold. You need to eat, and you can tell us what the hell all this is about."

Glynis slid the lamp from my grasp while Charlie turned me back around and led me to the little kitchenette table. "Are you even sure these are stolen coins? Have you seen a picture of them?"

"Well no," I answered, but they looked like they belong in a museum.

"Okay, let's start there." Glynis pulled out her phone and started typing. Her fingers slowed to a stop, and she turned the phone around. "Here's a picture of the coins from the paper when they were reported missing. There's a fifty thousand dollar reward for their return."

She turned the phone to me and the guys. The coins were identical to the ones that Charlie and Butler had.

I spent the next half-hour our telling them about the stolen coins between devouring two of the best-grilled cheese sandwich I've ever eaten. I pushed my plate away and drank my tea while Glynis, Charlie, and Butler sat in silence. Charlie had grabbed his coin and was staring down at it. "That explains your freak-out."

Butler sat forward, resting his elbows on his knees. "I don't get it. Logan told us that these coins have been in his family for centuries."

"That's not what he told me," Charlie interrupted. "Logan told me that he found them at an antique shop."

Glynis sat back and crossed her legs. "How many men do you know that go antiquing?"

The vibe in the room turned from disbelief to shock to somewhere around WTH.

"No way can you convince me that Logan helped steal those coins. There has to be another explanation." Butler rose and started pacing the floor.

"Maybe Davina gave them to him, and he just didn't know," Glynis said.

"Well, you guys realize there's one way to find out. Let's ask him." Charlie pulled out his phone. "I'll invite him over here." He glanced at me "Of course we'll stash Cree in the other room, but we'll just flat-out ask him. He'll tell us the truth."

"I don't know, guys. What if he sees me and tells his mother that I'm hiding out here? I don't have any way to defend myself besides the bedroom lamp. Everything I brought is in the cabana, and that's assuming that Priscilla hasn't destroyed it all. This isn't a good idea."

"I'd have to agree with Cree on this one. Do you honestly think Logan would have just given you guys stolen coins? He's smarter than that."

"Maybe he didn't know," Charlie said.

"The senator told me he threw a museum fundraiser here, and those coins were on display and he told both of you different stories. Of course, he knew," I said.

"Logan travels a lot for his job, and he hates having to attend his father's parties. He might have skipped that one," Butler said.

"What does he do for a living?"

"He's a computer genius. His company invented new security software that is one hundred percent safer than anything else on the market."

"He's in negotiations with several security firms that want the technology," Glynis announced.

If Logan knew his way around computer security, then he could have easily been involved in taking down the bank system. It made sense. Logan made sense.

"Call him and ask him to come over," I said, catching them each off guard. I'd be able to tell if he was lying by whether or not I got goosebumps from his answer.

"Are you sure?" Charlie asked.

"Yes. Like you said, I can hide in the other room."

"I'll hide with her," Glynis said.

"No, you need to go find your dad and tell him what happened with Priscilla. Maybe he can look for the gun that was used to kill Davina. Right now it's my word against hers unless we find some evidence."

"We'll take care of her," Charlie said, tossing his arm around my shoulder.

She gave me a hesitant look.

"I'll be fine, and I'll be gone as soon as the sun goes down."

She sighed and glanced around at the others. "Don't let him in that room."

"We won't," Butler promised. "Now go find your dad."

I peeked out the curtains in the bedroom. Night was coming fast. The ball was due to start in less than an hour. Butler had called Logan and asked him to come by his cabana for a drink with him and Charlie so they could go to the fundraiser together.

Charlie had gone back to his cabana to get dressed, and I tried to stay out of Butler's way while he got ready. I was helping with his cufflinks when there was a knock on the door. He shared a worried look as he walked out of the room and held my gaze as he pulled the bedroom door closed behind him.

I opened the door an inch to listen in on their conversation and pressed my back against the wall next to the door, in case someone walked in. The door would hide my presence.

"You're early," Butler said.

"The less time I have to spend at the fundraiser, the better. Where's Charlie?" This was a voice I hardly recognized. I peered through the edge of the door opening out into the room. The voice belonged to Logan all right. He looked just like I'd seen him during my Insight session.

"He's on his way. So what's your poison? I've got bourbon and tequila."

"Bourbon. That will help me make it through this damn fundraiser."

"I'm surprised you decided you let them talk you into attending. It can't be easy without Davina."

Ice clinked in a glass before Butler poured the liquor.

"They found her body," Logan announced out of the blue. "The police wanted to question my dad and me this morning. They confirmed she was pregnant."

"Man, I'm sorry. I couldn't imagine losing the woman I loved and an unborn child."

"It's been tough. Everyone has their own idea of trying to help me get through it, but all I see is a dark tunnel. There isn't a light. I'm just going through the motions trying to appear fine just so everyone will quit asking."

Goosebumps. Truth.

"I guess you should have kept those lucky coins you gave me and Charlie and used them for Davina and yourself."

That was a quick transition I hadn't been expecting.

"You aren't kidding."

"If you don't mind me asking, where did you get them from? I need to get one for my sister and the rest of the band."

I clenched my fist to my chest to try to calm my racing heart as I waited for him to answer.

"Davina said she and Clarissa found them on the beach."

Goosebumps. Regardless if it was true, he actually believed they'd found them on the beach.

"Then why the two lies about where they came from?" Butler asked.

He raised his brow. "Would you tell someone you didn't buy the present and that you got them for free?"

"This beach?"

"Yeah. Clarissa and Davina jog every morning even when we come to the island."

"I…ah…" There was a pause before Butler continued. "I didn't realize those two got along. I always thought Clarissa was jealous of Davina. She obviously had the hots for you for a long time."

"It was the other way around, dude. It was weird. They became thick as thieves like instant best friends that had known each other forever. They completed each other's sentences and everything. It was crazy weird, but I wasn't about to complain. I think they spent more time together that I did with either of them. I was always working, but my best friend and business partner should like my wife… well, almost wife."

"You didn't ask them if they knew each other before?"

Ice clinked in a cup, followed by more liquor being poured. "I caught them kissing once."

My eyes widened.

"You're shitting me."

"Nope, it was the night I met her. She was here at one of dad's fundraisers. It was right before Clarissa started hooking up with my dad."

"You knew about that?"

"Everyone on the island knows about their affair. They don't hide it very well."

"Does your mother know?"

There wasn't an answer. I could only imagine he shrugged.

"It's Clarissa." The words flew out of my mouth before I could stop them. My hand covered my mouth as the door was shoved open. I had to jump out of the way before getting smashed.

"Who the hell are you?"

"Cree Blue." My answer came out more like a question than an answer. "I have a story for you, Logan. One you aren't going to like but that you have a right to hear before the police show up."

"Butler, who is this woman?"

Butler walked into the room and took the empty glass from Logan's hand. "She's a psychic and a friend, Logan. She's the one who led police to Davina's body, and you really need to listen to what she has to say."

"You expect me to listen to a psychic? What the hell is this? Were you hoping she would tell me Davina is here and that I need to move on?"

"Actually she's not, but since you need proof." I took a deep breath. "Outside the church that last day, she told you she was going to get you a present and run errands."

"Anyone walking by could have heard that."

"You asked her if she was getting cold feet."

He turned silent, his face hard as stone.

"She reminded you that you promised her a do-over. Three boys and a house on a hill on the other side of the country away from your parents."

"That was our secret."

"I'm sorry for your loss, but that's not all I have to tell you." I gestured to the living room and for him to sit as Butler placed a drink in his hand.

I told him the story of how Davina had shown up and led me to her body and the cabin in the woods and the cash that I'd found. I told him how the feds figured out she worked at a bank where the coins were stolen and the security disabled. I'd explained how I uncovered his mother was responsible for shooting Davina, and how she threatened to kill me and locked me in the supply closet in her office. I told him everything, except that Davina had a previous affair with his dad. That part I left out because that part might have destroyed him.

By the time I was done, Logan was staring down at the coin Butler had handed him, and Logan's phone with the web page was open showing pictures of the missing coins.

He lifted his gaze. "My mother killed her?"

"I believe she did, but I haven't proved it. It's her word against mine, even though she admitted it to me when she locked me in the closet."

"Why?" He looked up at me. "Was it because of the affair Davina had with my dad?"

I shared a look with Butler, and he spoke. "You knew about that?"

He nodded. "Davina told me. She said she didn't want any secrets between us." He lifted the coin. "I guess she didn't mean *all* her secrets."

"Someone helped her disable the security at the bank. I thought it was you."

He shook his head and met my gaze. "You think Clarissa helped her?"

"I'm sorry, but I do. I just hadn't figured out their connection since Davina worked at a bank and Clarissa worked with computers."

He pressed his lips together. "I can answer that. I asked Clarissa where she'd met Davina the night I saw them kissing. She told me she met her awhile back at the bank where my company does business. I just didn't realize…"

I rested my hand over his. "Davina loved you. I believe she died wishing she'd told you the truth. I believe that she was going to the cabin that day to meet someone and had every intention of calling things off with whoever was waiting. I really believe she chose you."

Butler rested his palm on my shoulder. "Cree, it's dark enough. If you're going to make it to the boat, you should leave in the next few minutes. Freddie is going to be expecting you."

The door opened, and we all froze until Charlie walked in. "You're still here and talking to Logan, I see."

"You're involved in this?" Logan asked.

"I helped save her from the supply closet."

"My mother killed Davina."

"I heard. The police showed up. They just served a search warrant, and the police and FBI have converged on the hotel. They've confiscated your mother's rifles and handcuffed her. That's why I came down here. Harrison Reed, some big Italian scary-looking guy, and a cop named Faraday are looking for Cree."

"What about Clarissa?" I asked, slowly rising to my feet.

Logan rose from his seat. "They'll need proof that she hacked the bank's security the day the coins went missing. If she used her computer or one at the company, then I'll help them find the proof and the coins."

I used to feel vindicated when solving a case. I used to do it from the comfort of the Lady Blue. This case and these people were real, not some shady criminal who I'd expect to see in jail or at night scouring the streets for victims. I'd single-handedly pulled the rug out from beneath Logan's life. His mom was going to jail, his business partner was a thief, and his fiancée and baby were dead. How did one survive this type of aftermath?

Davina appeared in the room and held up her bear for me to see.

"Can I ask a question?"

"Sure."

"What was so special about the bear she had?"

He smiled for the first time since I met him. "Her mother gave her that bear the day she was born. It has a secret compartment in the back. She said that's where she kept her hopes, her wishes, and her dreams."

DEADLY VOWS

Chapter 17

It took two weeks for everything to settle down. Priscilla was arrested and held without bail.

The senator was dealing with the press, and Logan announced that Clarissa had left their security company days before she'd been arrested too.

Almost everything was right in my world again. West had been called away again but was due to return in a couple of weeks so we could start our case on Calinda Sparks and the missing diamond. I couldn't even fathom a guess at what was more urgent than working on Calinda's murder. It was just as well. Insight had been rewired, and I was hesitant to hook it back up and attach it to my head.

There was only one thing I had left to do. I stared up at the tall concrete building in front of me as men and women dressed casually came and went.

"I should have just mailed it," I whispered to myself as I pulled open the big door and headed toward the receptionist desk.

The receptionist smiled as I approached. "How can I help you?"

"I'd like to see Logan Channing, please."

"Do you have an appointment?"

"No, but if you could just tell him Cree Blue would like to speak to him and I'll only be a minute."

"Cree Blue?" she asked, rising from her seat. "You're the psychic responsible for Charlie turning down the movie deal?"

"Yes," I answered.

Her brow rose as she picked up the phone and hit some buttons. "Cree Blue is here to see you. She asked if you could spare a minute for her."

I couldn't hear the other end of the conversation, but I assume he agreed. The lady hung up the phone and handed me a badge. "Use that to swipe inside the elevators. Logan is on the top floor."

"Thank you." I smiled and headed for the elevator. I took it to the top. My stomach churned as Davina rode with me in silence. Her presence was still lingering, and until today, I had no idea why, but now I did. She still had unfinished business.

The elevator dinged, and I stepped off. Logan greeted me with an outstretched hand. "Well, this is a surprise."

"I hope I didn't catch you at a bad time."

"I would say I'm happy to see you, but the last time we met, my life turned upside down."

"Yeah, sorry about that. How are you holding up?"

"I'm a survivor, Ms. Blue. I'm dealing with it." He sounded sincere, but I knew deep down he was just putting on a show for me probably like he did for everyone else.

"It's okay to grieve. I'm sure your office will understand if you need to take some time," I said, taking a seat opposite his desk.

"I'm working on it," he said, sitting down. "I'm having to carry the load currently since Clarissa left the company."

"Did they ever find the coins?"

"Nope. She said Davina double-crossed her and hid the coins."

"You believe her?"

He shrugged. "The police searched both her and Davina's places from top to bottom and never found another coin. I did find proof on her computer that she took down the bank security system, so she's sitting in jail with my mother."

"You lost everything, didn't you? I'm so sorry."

"Yeah I did, but I'm trying to look at it as my own personal do-over. No matter Davina's flaws, all she wanted was to be happy. So I'm trying to take the same approach."

"I hope you find it."

"Me too." He smiled. "So what brings you by?"

"Davina hasn't moved on yet. She still has unfinished business."

He stared at me as if unsure what to say, so I continued. I pulled out the bear from my purse and rested it on his desk before retaking my seat. "She wanted you to have this."

He picked it up, and that was the first time I saw his facade slip. "Have you looked inside?"

"No. Whatever she placed inside was for you, not me or the police."

He ripped open the Velcro on the back and pulled out a picture. He turned to show it to me. It was a picture of him and Davina smiling with a beach in the background. That was his true smile in the picture, not the one he'd greeted me with.

"You two looked happy."

"We were." He pulled out two pieces of paper. He unfolded one, and a tear slipped down his cheek. He cleared his throat and began to read. "I didn't deserve you, but I loved you with every breath in my body and more than any riches I ever took. You're the only man that I gave my heart to in my entire broken life. I promise to love you forever."

"It's almost like she knew she was going to die."

He took a minute and a long deep breath before he set it down on the desk and unfolded the other piece of paper. His mouth parted as he stared at it. Any pain he was feeling was put on hold as he smiled. He turned it to face me. "She left me a treasure map."

"Where does it lead?"

"To the church. She wrote a note at the bottom. I didn't need the riches, all I needed was you."

"Wow. I guess that goes to show you she was going to choose you." I rose from my seat. "I should be going now."

I walked to the door when Logan spoke. "I loved her with every fiber of my soul."

I glanced back as I hit the elevator button. Davina was standing beside him with her hand covering her heart. "She loved you too."

I rode the elevator down in silence and ignored the whispers from the employees around me as I walked out of the building and to my car. I turned the ignition and turned up the radio as I pulled out heading home.

Calinda was in the seat beside me, grinning like she belonged. "It's almost time."

"I know," I answered and started down the road.

Butler's voice carried through my speakers. I'd recognize it anywhere as I listened to the radio interview about his latest single he was playing for the first time. I slowed to the side of the road around the same spot where my tire had gone flat.

"I'd like to dedicate this song to a very special lady. Cree Blue, here's a little *Soul Food* just for you."

The familiar strums of the guitar filled the air. His voice was silky smooth. I closed my eyes, and just for a moment, that minute in time, I just breathed in the calm serenity, letting it mend the frayed fragments of my own soul.

Car brakes squealed beside me, and I slowly opened my eye, my head lolling toward the intruder infringing on my solitude.

West rolled down his window. "What are you doing, luv?"

"Soothing my soul," I answered.

He pulled his car in front of me and got out. He held out his hand, making my brows dip.

"Take it," he prompted.

I slid my hand into his and let him pull me out of the Jeep. He held me close as he began to sway until the song died down and other music filled the air.

"That was unexpected."

"You were unexpected." He rested his hand on my cheek and lowered his lips to mine. He kissed me tenderly until the first rain drop fell, breaking our connection. I glanced up at the sky as our laughter filled the air.

"Is your soul soothed?" he asked as I hopped into my Jeep.

Thank goodness I'd kept the top on this time.

I glanced at Calinda. "It's getting there." I grinned. "Are you ready to get to work? Calinda has been waiting."

"Absolutely."

The End.

DEADLY VOWS

Thank you for spending time with Cree and her crew. There are several books coming soon in this series. If you enjoyed the book please consider leaving a review.

Next up is <u>Dead Famous</u> Release Date December 15, 2017

A dead actress. A missing diamond. A mystery left unsolved.

Psychic Cree Blue is at it again, and this promises to be her toughest case yet.

Normal people search for celebrities when they go to Hollywood. Cree Blue isn't normal. She's searching for a killer and a missing diamond whose ownership could change the destiny of a small country.

Given the mounting list of suspects and red-hot secrets with the potential to destroy lives, she's willing to risk it all to find the truth, even if that means immersing herself in the secret lives of

DEADLY VOWS

the rich and famous. Her only hope is that this trip to Tinsel Town doesn't steal her life too.

Keep reading for a taste of Dead Famous
Cree Blue Psychic Eye Book 3.

Chapter 1

I squeezed the pillow over my face. Death by suffocation would have been more tolerable than bleeding eardrums. It was six in the freakin' morning, and the obnoxious singing apparition haunting my room sounded like a million cats fighting over the last can of tuna.

I yanked the pillow off my face and turned my best evil-eye glare on the ghost floating across the room. Her designer ball gown didn't faze me, nor did the tiara on her head. It was the ongoing song she was belting out at the top of her voice that was grating on my last nerve. "Calinda Sparks, would you please just SHUT UP."

Calinda Sparks, the once famous, now dead movie star, was a constant annoyance in my life. Her stunning beauty and highly praised screen performances would never make up for the new sounds she was tormenting me with.

Okay, so maybe I *was* cranky, but who could blame me? This off-key dead actress needed to move into the light and out of my life.

She glanced at me and grinned as she floated across the room to stand over my bed. "People paid good money to hear me sing."

"Go haunt them instead," I grumbled and shoved the pillow back under my head. Rolling away from her, I closed my eyes and tried to get comfortable again. I still had four whole hours before I was needed downstairs. Four hours of dreaming of other things besides dead people, Brits, and my non-existent love life.

I closed my eyes and tried to let the dream world pull me back into its warm, inviting fold. The once lavish comforter felt itchy against my skin. The ticking of my alarm clock battling the crickets at my window continued now that the singing stopped. Both made my already pounding head hurt worse.

After thirty minutes of being unable to reclaim my perfectly good sleep, I just gave up. Today's lack of sleep promised I was going to be a grumpy hot mess, and I was blaming it all on the dead movie star.

****

I was on my second pot of coffee and cooking a proper southern breakfast my granny would have been proud of when John Faraday and Freddie entered the kitchen. They were quite the pair. The almost retired cop and ex-mobster were a constant presence in my house, and this was one of the mornings that I was thankful to have someone with a beating pulse to talk to.

They shared a concerned look as they entered. Faraday's cautious steps were almost as comical as when he rested his palm on my forehead.

"What are you doing?"

"I'm checking for a fever. Are you possessed?"

"I sure hope not. We can't cure possessed, and I'm positive I don't know any priest," Freddie, the ex-mobster, added.

I smiled and dished the eggs onto a platter and carried them into the dining room. "I wasn't possessed, but I was woken by a ghost who loves to listen to the sound of her own voice."

"Calinda has appeared again, has she?" West Archer asked walking into the kitchen; he stole a piece of bacon from the platter on my second pass.

Lord West Archer was my savior and a pain in my butt. He'd dangled Calinda's case in front of me to try and solve when the FBI had sent him my way. His disappearing and reappearing act was starting to give me whiplash-like a jolty ride at the carnival throwing me around creepy clowns. He was here now, though. I wasn't going to let him escape again unless Calinda Sparks promised to go with him. I'd never be that lucky, but a girl could hope, or maybe I could pay someone to invent a ghost blaster to send her off-key butt into the peaceful ever after.

I grabbed him by the lapels of his suit coat and wrinkled the material between my fingers. "She's driving me nuts and not in the cashew kind of way, the sucky kind of nuts that no one eats because they're healthy for you and lacking salt."

West's lips twisted at the corners, and he leaned in to kiss my cheek. "Find out who killed her and where she stashed the diamond and we can all enjoy the peace."

I smacked his arm. "I've tried asking, and she won't answer."

"Lucky you, I guess you're stuck with me a bit longer," he teased and followed me and the others into the dining room.

DEADLY VOWS

Sign up for her newsletters at www.kateallenton.com

Other Books by Kate Allenton

Suggested Reading Order
BENNETT SISTERS BOX SET (Books 1-4 in one bundle, 1218 pages)
BENNETT SISTERS BOX SET VOLUME 2 (Books 5-7 in one bundle, 517 pages}
INTUITION (Book 1)
TOUCH OF FATE (Book 2)
MIND PLAY (Book 3)
THE RECKONING (Book 4)
REDEMPTION (Book 5)
CHANCE ENCOUNTERS (Book 6)
DESTINED HEARTS (Book 7)

PHANTOM PROTECTORS BOX SET (Books 1-4 in one bundle, 964 pages)
RECKLESS ABANDON (Book 1)
BETRAYAL (Book 2)
UNTAMED (Book 3)
GUIDED LOYALTY (Book 4)

CARRINGTON-HILL INVESTIGATIONS
DECEPTION (Book 1)
DEADLY DESIRE (Book 2)

DEADLY VOWS

DEADLY VOWS

SHIFTER PARADISE BOX SET
NOT MY SHIFTER/ SINFULLY CURSED

KARMA

SOPHIE MASTERSON SERIES/ DIXON SECURITY
LIFTING THE VEIL (Book 1)
BEYOND THE VEIL (Book 2)
VEILED INTENTIONS (Book 3)
VEILED THREATS (Book 4)

THE LOVE FAMILY SERIES
SKYLAR (BOOK1)
DECLAN (BOOK 2)
FLYNN (BOOK 3)
REED (BOOK 4)
LANDON (BOOK 5)
ALEXIS (BOOK 6)
GABE (BOOK 7)
JACKSON (BOOK 8)

LINKED INC.
DEADLY INTENT (BOOK 1)
PSYCHIC LINK (BOOK 2)
PSYCHIC CHARM (BOOK 3)
PSYCHIC GAMES (BOOK 4)
DEADLY DREAMS (BOOK 5)

CREE BLUE PSYCHIC EYE

DEADLY VOWS

<u>DEAD WRONG</u> (BOOK 1)
<u>DEADLY VOWS</u> (BOOK 2)
<u>DEAD FAMOUS</u> (BOOK 3)
<u>DEADLY TIES</u> (BOOK 4)
<u>DEADLY BLISS</u> (BOOK5)

<u>HELL BOUND</u>
<u>MYSTIC TIDES BOX SET</u>
<u>MYSTIC LUCK BOX SET</u>
<u>MAID OF HONOR</u>
<u>HARD SHIFT</u>

DEADLY VOWS

About the Author

Kate has lived in Florida for most of her entire life. She enjoys a quiet life with her husband, Michael and two kids.

Kate has pulled all-nighters finishing her favorite books and also writing them. She says she'll sleep when she's dead or when her muse stops singing off key.

She loves creating worlds full of suspense, secrets, hunky men, kick ass heroines, steamy sex and oh yeah the love of a lifetime. Not to mention an occasional ghost and other supernatural talents thrown into the mix.
Sign up for her newsletters HERE
She loves to hear from her readers by email at KateAllenton@hotmail.com, on Twitter@KateAllenton, and on Facebook at facebook.com/kateallenton.1
Visit her website at www.kateallenton.com
Visit Coastal Escape Publishing's website at www.coastalescapepublishing.com